Begin the Beguine

Paul StJohn Mackintosh

Roswell Publishing

Text © 2023 Paul StJohn Mackintosh and Roswell Publishing.

The rights of Paul StJohn Mackintosh identified as the originator of this work has been asserted by them in accordance with the Copyright, Designs and Patents Act 1988.

All rights reserved. No part of this publication may be reproduced, stored in a retrieval system, or transmitted in any form or by any means electronic, mechanical, photocopying, recording or otherwise, without prior permission.

ISBN: 9798866762613

Cover image: Sophia Conner

For rights and other permissions, please contact Rachael at: rae@raegee.co.uk

Preface

I'm sure the genesis of this novel will be obvious once you spot the connections and parallels. It was originally conceived in a spirit of reverence towards the mighty figures of the earlier 20th century, inspired in part by my maternal grandfather, George A. Wheatcroft, who served in the Royal Engineers in the Western Desert during World War 2, and later became President of the International Optometric and Optical League. In among my second-hand nostalgia for that period, I'd always admired the "polished, urbane and adult" songs of Cole Porter. Casually perusing the compositional history of "Begin the Beguine," I then came across Artie Shaw, and discovered what a remarkable Renaissance man he was – star jazz clarinettist, writer, marksman, amateur mathematician, and serial husband of a succession of dazzling women. Plus, the song's title had stuck in my head for a long time thanks to Max Beckmann's painting of the same name, which made me think that there must be stranger, darker depths to the song and its period. And when I discovered that Cole Porter had begun writing "Begin the Beguine" aboard the RMS *Franconia* in Indonesian waters, inspired by his contact with Asian music, and that Artie Shaw had later turned it into one of the great hits of the wartime swing era, *and* that Winston Churchill had enlisted the *Franconia* as his floating headquarters during the Yalta Conference, the whole story practically fell together by itself. The revelation of Artie Shaw's son Jonathan, the real living celebrity tattooist, and the story of his cache of firearms was the final touch needed to top off the whole thing.

   Some major themes of the narrative should be obvious from the start: the passing of Western predominance over the globe, the timely end to the era of European colonialism solemnized at Yalta, Scotland's equivocal position as victim and enabler of English imperialism, the handoff of Western culture and especially musical culture to non-Western traditions, the advent of mass culture and mass hysteria, and so on. World War 2 itself is still the founding epic of our times, and I wanted to memorialize Scotland's role in that conflict and all that led up to it, not least the tragedy of the bombing of Clydebank. There are also a lot of memories of Asia in here, and yearning for the places I hadn't seen in almost a decade.

I might apologize to readers who don't like data dumps for the structure of this novel, but let me explain briefly. The factual details and minutiae in this story are not informational: any reader nowadays can find almost all this information online – that's what I did. For the same reason, they're certainly not intended to impress or overawe anyone. They're there as triggers for the imagination, in the same way that Tom Clancy militarese or sci-fi technobabble does. E.L. Doctorow's *Ragtime* helped confirm my confidence in this approach – and in the entire approach to the novel – but it also comes from my genre fiction background. I see no reason that "serious" literature should give up the imaginative and immersive triggers that genre fiction relies on to absorb readers in the story, and I also believe that those details function for world-building in a historical or contemporary novel, in the same way that imagined names do in fantasy. (A certain public constituency clings to this shelf in the set-dressing wardrobe as "real" and "true," but at the end of the day, these are all equally works of the imagination.) So that's what the details are for. Hayao Miyazaki helped to confirm this approach too, by implanting mechanical creations right in the centre of his wonderful fantasies: the *Franconia* in this story owes plenty to the planes of *Porco Rosso* and Lord Howl's Moving Castle. I won't pretend that, like Mozart or Cole Porter, I could make this laundry list of nuts and bolts sing, but I've tried not to let it drag too much.

I also follow Joseph Conrad's dictum, articulated in the author's note to *The Shadow Line* added to the second edition in 1920, that the everyday world "in all conscience holds enough mystery and terror in itself" to obviate any need to double down with the supernatural and fantastic. With that, though, I also follow Jorge Luis Borges's spin on this in the

Paris Review: "Conrad thought that when one wrote, even in a realistic way, about the world, one was writing a fantastic story because the world itself is fantastic and unfathomable and mysterious." Borges then quotes his friend and collaborator Adolfo Bioy Casares declaring: "I think Conrad is right. Really, nobody knows whether the world is realistic or fantastic, that is to say, whether the world is a natural process or whether it is a kind of dream, a dream that we may or may not share with others." Whatever Conrad actually thought, that's my approach to the historical (or "real world") novel, and its relationship to other genres – all of them equally fantastic and imaginative, because in the end, there is plenty of fiction that is not realistic, but none that is not imaginative. I am utterly opposed to naturalism, in literature or philosophy, and this novel is absolutely not naturalistic, closer to Max Beckmann than Meredith Frampton in its depiction of an era and its signature tune.

My grateful thanks to Jonathan Shaw for his approval for this book, and for his appearance in it. My thanks also to the University of Liverpool for access to the Cunard Archive, to the Clydebank Local History Society, and to the naval history enthusiasts who maintain the uboat.net website, which helped with a lot of the wartime details. FantasyCon 2019 unexpectedly landed me on the spot in Clydebank itself while I was working on the novel – as serendipitous a happenstance as any writer could wish for. Thanks also to Rae, my publisher, for actually recognizing this work, and to Krys, my editor and my best critic. My thanks to my parents and my family for being who they are, and my daughters for being who they are – my best achievements. Finally, thanks always to bast for being who she is.

- Paul StJohn Mackintosh, 2023

Chapter 1

It's early November in the second year of Barack Obama's first term when the bust goes down. The NYPD has been called to the premises of a shipping company on 10th Avenue, where the workers have accidentally opened a shipment booked by Jonathan Shaw, celebrity tattoo artist and son of former star bandleader Artie Shaw. One of the movers lifts a vintage 1950s suitcase by its handle, which breaks off, revealing a bullet inside. Alarmed, the workers open it and investigated further. The suitcase was filled with ammunition. As soon as he's notified, the shipping company CEO orders a lockdown of the facility, and goes through the shipment in detail, discovering some weapons in another duffle bag. Immediately he calls the police.

Shaw's shipment, once fully itemized, contains a Norinco AK-47 assault rifle with a fully loaded half-moon magazine, a Mossberg 12-gauge pistol-grip shotgun, a loaded World War 2 M1 Garand .30-calibre carbine, a loaded Lee Enfield .303 SMLE rifle of similar vintage, an air rifle, five blank-firing handguns, 96 knives including a gravity knife and switchblades, five sets of brass knuckles, eight collapsible batons, two blackjacks, and nearly 3,000 rounds of ammunition. The NYPD are cautious – after all, they're dealing with a potential multiple weapons felony. Plus, Jonathan Shaw is a celebrity of sorts, tattooist to the stars, friend of Iggy Pop, Kate Moss, Jean-Michel Basquiat, and all kinds of other wild and crazy figures, allegedly Johnny Depp's inspiration for the character of Jack Sparrow in *Pirates of the Caribbean*. His tattoo parlour, Fun City on St. Mark's Street in the East Village, was a mini-Mecca back in the days of the nascent New York punk and hardcore scenes, before he sold it off in 2004. The NYPD are used to handling media cases, but they don't want to court publicity – or tangle with influential and unconventional people.

For all their caution, the NYPD's first moves don't go so well. They trace Shaw to an apartment registered in his name in the

West Village, and attempt to arrest the occupant. It isn't Shaw, just some ordinary Joe whose girlfriend did some work for Shaw. They leave after the girlfriend convinces them that they have the wrong guy. Then the police track Shaw down to his suite at the Hotel Roger Williams at 131 Madison Avenue. It doesn't seem like his natural turf; swank Midtown surroundings, very different from his longtime East Village haunts. They try to lure him back to his cache. An NYPD detective calls Shaw around midnight, posing as a mover from the shipping company, reporting that his goods have been accidentally damaged. Shaw doesn't take the bait, and hangs up. (Later he claims that his P.A. called him and tipped him off.) At 2:00 a.m., the police arrive at his hotel – named after the Rhode Island Puritan theologian and abolitionist, with the elegant "131" over its front entrance – and arrest Shaw. He does not resist.

Shaw is arraigned in Manhattan Criminal Court, charged with two counts of second-degree criminal weapons possession, 113 third-degree counts of criminal possession of a weapon, one count of possession of a shotgun, one count of unlawful possession of ammunition, and one count of possession of air pistols and air rifles. The assistant DA asks for $300,000 bond or $150,000 cash bail, claiming that Shaw is a serious flight risk, facing a significant prison term. Shaw's lawyer states that his client had legally purchased the weapons over 15 years ago in the state, and had documentation for all of them. He also states that Shaw now lives on the West Coast, and is only in New York to help a friend put on an exhibition at the Jewish Museum. Shaw leaves court after posting bond of $250,000, with no comment to waiting reporters.

Shaw appears in court the following January, pleading not guilty to the firearms charges, and evades further prosecution. Once again, he makes no comment to journalists. He doesn't reveal that the M1 Garand and the .303 rifle were gifts from his father, himself a precision marksman, rated one of the country's best shots in the early 1960s. He doesn't reveal the whole story behind the rifles, because he doesn't know it himself. The few who did know that story were sworn to secrecy long ago. It's a long and complicated story, with many interweaving threads. To understand it, you have to know a lot about the people involved, and the times they lived through. But it's a story worth the telling, and all the hard work, as all good stories are.

Chapter 2

The RMS *Franconia* is a Cunard Line ocean liner, built on Clydebank by John Brown & Company, launched on 21 October 1922. She is a successor to Cunard's first RMS *Franconia*, launched on 23 July 1910, ironically named after a region in central Germany, and sunk by a German torpedo on 4 October 1916. She has a gross registered tonnage of 20,175 tons, at roughly 600 feet in length and 73 feet across her beam. Powered by six steam turbines with a shaft horsepower of 13,500 SHP, she is capable of 16.5 knots, a stately pace that will make a great difference later on.

   Cunard has been struggling in the immediate post-war years, and needs new ships. The first *Franconia* was one of eleven ships lost to German attacks during World War 1, including the *Lusitania*, leaving only eight liners in service. Replacements from the Hamburg America Line and other spoils of war are nowhere near enough to make up the losses, so Cunard begins a new building programme to add 14 ships to the fleet. This is more than just a private business matter: the great intercontinental shipping lines are important strategic assets, the thews of Empire, and the great liners have already proven their naval worth during the Great War, with commensurate casualties to show for it. Still, Cunard, that grand dame of shipping lines, whose recently-completed Cunard Building, third of Liverpool's Three Graces, shines out above George's Pier Head in her home port, is short of money post-war, and can't afford to match the pre-war superliners on the scale of the *Mauretania, Lusitania* and *Aquitania*, with their four funnels. Instead, the Cunard Board opts for smaller vessels to make up the lost tonnage. After the first few single-stack designs, they raise their sights somewhat for the *Franconia*, and commission Leonard Peskett, Cunard head designer and creator of the legendary *Aquitania* – the "Ship Beautiful" – to produce a particularly elegant specimen of naval architecture. His success is soon apparent. The *Franconia* has fabulous interiors, two garden lounges, a Renaissance smoking room, a health spa, a

Pompeian swimming pool, and a squash and racketball court. Her decks are laid out to afford the maximum open space for deck sports, dances, promenades, trap shooting and other amusements en voyage. Her regular staterooms boast an unusually large floor area by the standards of the day, while her larger suites rival any five-star hotel on land. Her amenities include a library and writing room, a confectionery, a barber's shop and a hair salon, a dental parlour, and a miniature hospital. Leisure cruises, a fashionable novelty just before the Great War, are now coming into their own as major money-spinners for the shipping lines in the off-seasons for passenger traffic. Cunard has seen the potential for dual-purpose passenger liners that can double as luxury cruise ships during the slack periods for the regular transatlantic routes, and the *Franconia* is the fulfilment of that vision. What she lacks in palatial scale, she makes up for in sheer elegance.

Registered in the Cunard home port of Liverpool, the *Franconia* is launched on 21 October 1922 by Lady Royden, wife of Cunard chairman Sir Thomas Royden, and makes her maiden voyage in 23 June 1923, on the Liverpool-to-New York run which becomes her regular summer passage. She's painted in the Cunard colours: red funnel with a black band at the top and thin black rings; golden brown "mast colour" masts and derricks; white superstructure, boats and ventilators; black hull. With a crew of over 400, she can carry some 220 first-class, 340 second-class and 1,260 third-class passengers on these transatlantic trips, but she becomes especially associated with luxury round-the-world cruises in the winter months, catering to a far more select passenger list of around 400.

Cunard has forged a new pre-eminence by offering the first ever complete round-the-world voyages by cruise liner, and winter trips offer the best schedule for a clientele eager to escape the chill of northern winters, yet preferring to experience tropical climes in their most tolerable seasons. The most splendid first-class two-person suites for these cruises fetch some $25,000, with all onshore charges included – rail travel, motor or carriage excursions, hotel accommodation onshore, landing and embarkation charges, and the services of local interpreters and guides. The *Franconia* is so successful as a cruise liner that more and more of her sailing time is devoted to such voyages, on various itineraries. She suffers only a couple of minor accidents during the Twenties – somewhat prophetic of her later war career. In December 1926, she accidentally runs aground in San Juan harbour, and is refloated a few days later; then in April 1929, she accidentally collides in Shanghai harbour with an Italian gunboat and a Japanese tramp steamer. Her propellers become entangled with a small buoy, and in the ensuing confusion, a lighter is sunk and four of its crew drowned.

   The typical itinerary of one of the *Franconia*'s five-month round-the-world cruises, departing from New York, takes in Havana and Panama, then through the Canal to San Francisco, across the Pacific via Honolulu to Yokohama and Kobe, across the South China Sea to Shanghai, Hong Kong, Manila, Batavia and Singapore, then into the Indian Ocean with stops at Rangoon, Calcutta and Colombo, up the Arabian Sea via Bombay to the Red Sea via Port Sudan, Cairo and Suez, then into the Mediterranean with further stops at Alexandria, Monaco and Gibraltar, before the final ten-day Transatlantic crossing back to New York. En route, passengers can drive to the active crater of Kilauea, ride rickshaws through the Shanghai International Settlement, scale Victoria Peak, explore the Island of Elephanta, pay homage to the Sphinx and the Pyramids, delve in the blasted ruins of Pompeii, steam to the Blue Grotto, and play the tables at Monte Carlo. Optional excursions range even further, to Mount Fuji and the Forbidden City, the Taj Mahal and the ghats of Benares, the tombs of Luxor and the Holy Sepulchre. By the 1930s, this itinerary has been varied and expanded to take in Java, Fiji and Australia, and her round-the-world voyages are a globetrotting legend. Initially sporting a black lower hull in typical Cunard trim, by 1935 she has been repainted entirely in heat-resistant white.

   The *Franconia* sails on through the Great Depression, despite reduced traffic across the North Atlantic, and increased competition from Italian and German prestige liners. The 1934 merger between Cunard and White Star Line, the residue of John Pierpont Morgan's pre-war market-rigging efforts, leaves her untouched, although many of her sister ships, the *Mauretania*, the *Olympic* and the *Homeric*, go to the scrapyard. She retains her status as a shining icon of luxury and prestige against the increasingly darker backdrop of the 1930s. And one of her crew is the Clydebank native, John Graham.

Chapter 3

Growing up on Clydebank in the early 20th century means growing up in the shadow of ships. So it's no surprise that John Graham ends up serving in one.

John Graham is born in 1910, fourth son of a sprawling family that claims descent from the martyr hero James Graham, the Great Montrose. By 1910, needless to say, the family has come a long way down in the world, although nowhere near as low as the poor uprooted casualties of the Clearances, hoarded into the Glasgow slums to feed the Molochs of Caledonian industry. His father, Alistair Graham, is lower middle class, a technical draughtsman at the great firm of John Brown & Company, which bought the shipyard that created the town of Clydebank from its Scottish owners in 1899. John Brown & Company has made the iron cladding for Royal Navy warships since the 1860s, and the company's move into Scotland marks its transition from steelmaking to actual shipbuilding. The Graham family, like most of Clydebank, depend on the fortunes of John Brown – "John Broon," as John grows up hearing it – and the Singer sewing machine works next door. And they depend so closely and completely on the great Clyde-buit Cunarders, the *Lusitania* and *Aquitania*, that those hulls are practically the cradles that John is rocked in.

Clydebank also owes much to Cunard, and its close association with British Imperial power and prestige. The first great fillip for John Brown in its new line of business and its new location comes with Cunard's commissioning of two great liners, paid for by a British government loan of £2.6 million, agreed in 1903, repayable by Cunard over 20 years at only 2.75% interest, with a further annual government operating subsidy of £75,000 for each ship, plus a mail contract worth £68,000. The terms of the loan agreement involve the Admiralty heavily in the design of the ships, as both are to be built to naval specifications, so they can be used as auxiliary cruisers during wartime.

Prestige and power politics trump private enterprise, yet Cunard and the British government aren't the only guilty parties in this rigged struggle. The great German shipping lines Norddeutscher Lloyd and Hamburg America Line, supported by the expanding German Empire, have outbuilt and outrun the Cunarders, with multiple Blue Riband wins for the fastest Atlantic crossing. Meanwhile, the American plutocrat J.P. Morgan has folded his British shipping interests into his International Mercantile Marine (IMM) conglomerate, and formed a price-fixing cartel with the German lines in 1902 to control the transatlantic trade.

Cunard takes the unprecedented step of designing its first vessel for the fightback, soon dubbed the *Lusitania*, around steam turbine engines, little used so far in civilian craft. The Admiralty tests her hull design in their experimental tanks, refining and streamlining her, and their requirements put all her machinery below the waterline, and coal bunkers along her length for added protection against attack. Above the waterline, though, Cunard goes to town to create the most stupendous, luxurious ship of the age. Six passenger decks instead of the usual four. Plasterwork interiors from the Scottish architect James Miller. A two-deck first class dining saloon decorated with rococo frescoes. A Georgian style first class lounge with mahogany panels, a barrel vaulted skylight and stained glass windows. Wireless telegraph, electric lighting and lifts, and what passes in that age for air conditioning. Even the third class accommodation is a notable advance on previous arrangements for that class of passenger, with cabins instead of dormitories.

The *Lusitania*'s keel is laid down at John Brown on Clydebank 16 June 1904 as yard no. 367. Cunard dubs her "the Scottish ship." Lord Inverclyde, the Cunard chairman responsible for securing the government loans, hammers her first rivet. The whole shipyard is reorganized around her to accommodate the construction and launch of a ship of such unprecedented length. At launch, she is the largest ship ever built, though eclipsed soon after by her sister ship, the *Mauretania*. The work involved in her construction, and all the supporting design and drafting, provides steady employment and financial stability for Alistair Graham and his new family, for he has just wed Louise Kelly, a factory girl from the Singer Sewing Machine factory next door.

Unusually, it's a mixed marriage: although conformist and properly Presbyterian in most other walks of his life, Alistair Graham, like many other Scots before him, lets passion overrule his usual prudence, and weds the girl of his heart. Louise's Catholicism makes little impression on family life. She is content with a good responsible husband who has taken her out of the drudgery of the Singer sewing works. An elder sister and three elder brothers follow before John's birth.

John Brown wins the competitive tender for the construction of the RMS *Aquitania*, laid down in December 1910, reassuring Alistair that he will have steady employment to support his growing family. She's an even grander vessel than her predecessor: broader in the beam than the greyhound-like *Lusitania*, and the first Cunarder over 900 feet in length. Her first class interiors are even grander and more spacious than the *Lusitania*, designed by the same firm that decorated the London and Paris Ritz. She has a Palladian first class lounge, a Carolean smoking room with a T-shaped Admiral's Walk, and eight luxurious first-class suites named after great painters. Thanks to the recent sinking of the *Titanic*, she also has a double hull divided into watertight compartments, and is one of the first liners to launch with enough lifeboats for all her passengers and crew. One of John Graham's first memories is being taken round the ship by his proud father prior to her launch in April 1913, toddling on her teak upper decks in the shadow of her towering masts and funnels. The scent of deck polish is added to the salt tang of the sea, the grey smell of rain when it "pishes down," and the mercaptan reek of town gas in his childhood repertoire of formative odours. Otherwise, his world is defined by the Town Hall, the Police Station, the Swimming Baths, and the great gates of the shipyard, watched over by local colossi like the 150-foot Titan Crane, the world's largest cantilever crane, and the mighty Singer clock tower with its huge gilt SINGER letters above all four faces.

The outbreak of war in August 1914 brings even more security and prosperity to the Graham family, for the yards of Clydebank will be kept thrumming to support the war at sea, and Alistair is employed in a crucial war industry, with skills essential to the national effort, and no danger of being called up. The elder Grahams are all just too young to serve, no matter how eagerly they follow the news from the Front and want to join the colours. Local efforts like the Titan Crane, which builds 47 ships, are their substitutes for heroism. Not that that makes much impression on young John, huddled under broad dusty leaves in the kitchen garden, gnawing the rhubarb stalks, savouring the bitter sting from the pinky stems. For all the tough reputation of Clydeside, it's almost an idyllic childhood: running and boating in newly-built Dalmuir Park, mingling in the often rough-edged but by no means uncultured or uneducated lower-middle-class society of Greater Glasgow. There's little traffic in those days, and often he's found outside on Dumbarton Road or Hall Street, playing with the other Bankie kids, until the five o'clock siren signals the end of the working day and the stampede of shipwrights released by the opening of the shipyard gates. John's a thoughtful boy, and a rather precious and pampered one, beneficiary of his siblings' protection and apple of his mother's eye. He doesn't run round the park waving tomahawks made from branches and flattened soup cans like the other kids. At his mother's prompting, his father gets him a hot-water bottle, a great copper thing handmade by one of the joiners at the yard, to make sure he keeps his strength up and fights off the diseases still too prevalent in Glasgow.

Like most Bankie kids, John goes to Clydebank School. The rather formidable new building on Kilbowie Road is a zoo, overcrowded to almost double its capacity with the children of war workers drafted in to serve the common struggle. It's hardly an environment for solid study, but John manages somehow, helped by his father's devotion to learning. Clydebank Library becomes one of his other regular ports of call, and he devours the work of Walter Scott, Robert Louis Stevenson and Arthur Conan Doyle along with the other schoolboy fare of the period, feeding his nascent wanderlust, and his yen to see foreign places and wider horizons.

John loses many of his friends with the end of the War, when the massive draft of war workers and their families begins to trickle away, and he's still there in 1921 when the new High School is split off from the original institution. It's a relatively high-quality foundation by its lights, with strong morale, a proper uniform with school colours of chocolate and gold, and a Caledonian dedication to self-improvement and advancement through scholarship. All the boys wear their school ties, though the dress code for the girls is less strict, and not all of them wear pigtails for the boys to pull. John shows most promise in mathematics and technical subjects, and it looks like he's going to follow the path of many a capable Scottish boy, and pursue a career in the sciences or engineering. His mother is inordinately proud of the prizes he brings home, although she wouldn't claim to understand their subjects. The question of university doesn't arise, though; John's father is a proud practitioner of a technical trade, and doesn't want to hear of his son wasting time on such highbrow stuff; besides, his star is already leading in quite a different direction.

John follows the usual course for a young Briton with serious maritime ambitions but no family pedigree of naval service: at age 17, he applies for a four-year apprenticeship with the Cunard Line at £8 per month, with the intent of eventually passing his second mate's exams and becoming a ship's officer. He's already picked up some maritime training with the Sea Cadets, joining the Dalmuir Junior Cadets at age 11, and has his basic boatwork, target-shooting, navigation and seamanship skills down pat. Naturally he's hoping for one of the glamour postings for his first berth, especially given the family's association with Cunard's favourite shipyard, but he's assigned to the RMS *Alaunia*, an intermediate liner built to keep fuel bills low and launched just two years before his engagement, named after a predecessor lost to a wartime mine. The *Alaunia* is a solid enough vessel, almost 540 feet long and 65 feet in the beam, with room for 500 cabin passengers, and 1,200 in third class, flying Cunard's golden lion rampant on a red ground holding a golden globe – very soon joined after the merger by the White Star Line's white star on its red burgee. She's kept busy primarily on the transatlantic passenger service, from Southampton to Quebec and Montreal in the summer, and Halifax in the winter. Aboard her, he learns his trade, as a standard ordinary seaman, bunking and messing with the deck crew in steel bunks along the bulkheads. He even has to buy his own uniform – a more tolerable expense for his family than for some of his messmates. He works long hours, usually 7:00 a.m. to 10:00 p.m, under a heavy workload and stern discipline, all according to the Cunard *Rule Book for Crew*. It's two years of cleaning bilges, restoring paintwork and polishing brass, washing out freshwater tanks, and holystoning teak decks, chipping ice off the superstructure during the coldest crossings, all under the stern guidance of the bosun. He learns the habits of the transatlantic service: the jealously guarded seaman's locker full of home remedies against the chills and ailments of the voyage; the almost silent breakfasts together. The passengers are a motley bunch, given the ship's focus on convenience rather than luxury, but that's hardly his affair. As an ordinary member of the deck crew, he's not supposed to fraternize with them anyway, and the passenger spaces are usually forbidden him.

   The *Alaunia* might or might not be a lucky ship, but in any event she's lucky for him, with no major collisions or upsets during his service aboard her. After two years, he makes able seaman, and passes his lifeboatman qualification. He stands watches on the bridge in uniform, as helmsman and lookout. He maintains the almost teetotal abstinence of a navigating officer at sea with little difficulty, thanks to that streak of Glasgow puritanism he picked up from his father. Otherwise, the same old routine of chipping and painting, maintenance and cleaning, continues. He spends more time as a day worker in the deck department, but this entails plenty of additional work on the superstructure, lifeboats and small craft, and the ship's funnel. At least there he feels like he's doing a real seaman's job, unlike the glorified waiters in the steward's department, waiting on the droves of emigrants to Canada. The navigating officers on a smaller liner like the *Alaunia* are a tight-knit bunch of a dozen or so, and the deck department not many more in proportion to the service department, but they retain that spirit of a class apart. It's a pernicious discrimination, he knows, that saps a ship's morale, but he can't help feeling it. After two more years of studying navigation and seamanship, he passes his exams to become a third mate.

John makes it through the difficult early years of the Great Depression, when shipping worldwide hits a downturn and many crews are laid off. Cunard keeps him in limbo for an awkward year, on a lower salary, when he's sent to continue his training with the Royal Navy aboard an obsolete cruiser, gaining the rank of lieutenant in the Royal Naval Reserve. At the end of this time, instead of the sack, he gets a reposting to the RMS *Franconia*. Cunard has fared better than the White Star Line, and is busy absorbing its moribund competitor into a joint fleet that it fully controls. That grand old lady the *Mauretania*, and many of her pre-war generation, are deemed surplus to requirements and broken up, but the *Franconia*, built post-war, is fully up to the challenge of inter-war speeds and standards. The Cunard/White Star merger means that higher salaries are impossible, but at least the ships, and the work, are there. John's luck has held once again, and his career is destined to remain afloat.

It's a very different world now for the young seaman, though. Instead of the workmanlike merchant marine duties aboard the *Alaunia*, he's now expected to keep up standards of dress and decorum appropriate to a luxury liner ferrying the elite to the world's most glamorous and exotic destinations. The *Franconia* plies the Liverpool-New York run in the summer months, carrying the same gaggle of picturesque, polyglot migrants bound for the New World, but in the winter she heads south along routes designed to offer high-paying passengers their fill of winter sunshine. Perforce, John becomes more of a blue-water sailor, trading the cold grey seas of the North Atlantic, and the England that Stevenson once dismissed as a nasty cold muddy hole with not enough light to see to read by, for the tropical sapphire gleam of the Indian Ocean and the South Pacific. For a Scot, it's a revelation. His early memories of Stevenson's *The Wrecker, The Ebb-Tide* and *Island Nights' Entertainments* come flooding back, and for a while he's voyaging once again through the enchanted oceans of boyhood. It's hard to feel too romantic at the best of times about the Southampton to Halifax run, but now he is sailing in a white swan across mother-of-pearl seascapes, convoyed by rose-pink cloud argosies that tower thousands of feet above tropic calms. So what if the now-familiar wharves of Hong Kong, Singapore, Bombay and Java are as filthy and squalid as any port in the globe, once seen close up? John is experiencing the epiphany that many another Northerner, their expectations and impressions pre-emptively pinched by dark and narrow latitudes, has stumbled upon before him: that the world is a vastly wider, richer, brighter, more fecund, more overwhelming place than he ever could have imagined. Colours and smells press in on his newly sensitized awareness: flame trees, red sealing wax palms, hibiscus, azalea, orchid. Sweat and sunburn, damp and rot, it's all part of the savour of the same delicious cocktail.

On board, it's a new world too. John glories in the power and grace of his new home, her speed and her elegance. No matter how workmanlike the arrangements for the deck crew, he can't ignore the fact that he's now surrounded by undreamt-of opulence – wooden panelling, ornate doors, polished silver, crisp table linen, stewards and waiters dressed and drilled as punctiliously as in any grand manor. He can eat in the first class dining saloon, albeit at the separate table for the deck officers, positioned where they can slip away discreetly in case of any emergency. Lobsters, oysters and caviare become part of his daily fare, even when snatched on the run in the ship's galley. The rigid hierarchies of the crew, the pervasive consciousness of rank and status, somehow seem more bearable, even natural, in this context, part of the onus on Cunard men to keep up the Company's reputation for decorum and punctilio in competition with the other lines. Without realizing it, John picks up the ability to mix with millionaires while not losing the common touch. Vicariously, he's been admitted to the company of the upper classes, not quite below stairs, somewhat at arm's length, rather like a trusted family solicitor or doctor – a congenial role for a Scot.

With his third mate's licence, John is rated Junior Third Officer of the *Franconia*, fifth in line of command of the vessel and chief safety officer, overseeing ship's operations, emergency preparations, sea watch and navigation. Serving only four hours on the bridge, with the Chief Officer and quartermasters, and eight hours off, he has more time for study. The immense complexities of the liner's complement, its hundreds of ancillary and specialist staff, are almost all outside his area of responsibility, and he has time to concentrate on his seamanship. He develops a special aptitude for two disciplines: navigation and the operation of small craft. With his scientific bent, he eagerly absorbs the principles of celestial, terrestrial and coastal navigation, the intricacies of Sailing Directions and tide tables, the orchestration of winds and currents. That feel for the interplay of forces prevailing at sea weaves into his competence with small boats, both in handling them inshore and in managing them on board ship. Even the usual Junior Third Officer's duties of overseeing the stern ropes at arrival and departure help him broaden his understanding of the shallows and currents at each port they moor in. He oversees many lifeboat drills without a single slip or accidental injury, winning the Cunard challenge cup for excellence in the drill. He becomes chief pilot and leader for shore parties, and those excursions when passengers are taken ashore by ship's boats. That needs a certain touch with the passengers as well as the helm, but fortunately, John rises to the occasion. The sailing officers on a Cunarder are not expected to fraternize with the passengers, neither to drink with them socially nor to visit their cabins, but in John's case, contact is unavoidable, and fortunately, something he carries off easily. As Commodore Arthur Rostron the veteran Cunarder once remarked, all Cunard ships have three sides – port, starboard and social – and a Cunard officer must be master of them all, be polite and helpful to the passengers without ever crossing that bar into undue familiarity.

The quiet, thoughtful, personable young Scot, innocent of English caste consciousness, manages the guests deftly and courteously, and makes a good impression on princes and plutocrats alike. That dual competence would normally mark him for advancement at Cunard, and his senior officers begin to look on him with greater favour. He enjoys answering the occasional nautical and geographical questions from passengers on the promenade deck, and broadens his knowledge to do so. He's not much of a sportsman, but he's popular with his crewmates. He contributes a few articles on navigation and practice in port to the *Franconia's* crew magazine, *The Commodore*. No prig, he still diligently attends Divine Service every Sunday, conducted in the first-class salon by the captain. The Character Book where the line keeps note of his personal qualities rates him highly for intelligence, sobriety, education, and readiness for promotion. It's then that he encounters Cole Porter.

Chapter 4

You'd never expect someone with a background like Cole Porter's to become the balladeer of his age. But the creative gift will transcend class and race boundaries to cross the globe and touch hearts everywhere, universal.

Cole Porter is born in 1891 into the glitter of the Gilded Age. Hailing from Peru, Indiana, his family can't quite claim to be part of Oliver Wendell Holmes's "Brahmin Caste of New England," but they boast more than enough wealth and prestige to be counted among the national elite, especially in the person of Cole's maternal grandfather, James Omar (J.O.) Cole, the quintessential American self-made entrepreneur, styled Indiana's richest man. In his pictures as in his name, J.O. looks just a single initial away in form and spirit from his august contemporary, J.P. Morgan. J.O. is a dominating presence in Cole's boyhood, not least since his mother, Kate Cole, has married somewhat beneath her, to a shy, diffident local druggist, Samuel Fenwick Porter. J.O has pampered his cherished daughter all her life, and determines that she should continue to enjoy the standard of living to which she has been accustomed. He subsidizes and supports the young family, paying for their wedding, and building them a home on his property, Westleigh Farms – a pillared, porticoed "farmhouse" that would not look out of place at the heart of an antebellum Southern plantation. J.O's munificence, and his expectations, define Cole's youth, just as his grandfather has already determined his name.

Kate herself is no cipher, evidently inheriting much of the Cole grit that took her father from his origins as a humble shoemaker's son to the dry goods trade during the California gold rush, through coal and timber speculation, to the top tier of Indiana society. She is musical and cultivated to a more than ornamental degree, and lavishes her attentions on her only son with all the dedication of a mother spoiled and indulged throughout her own childhood. At her insistence, Cole begins learning the violin at age six, soon following this with the piano. His mother keeps him practising the piano for two hours a day, but helps out her young son's concentration by parodying then-popular tunes for him. Under her tutelage, his musical gift blossoms. At age ten, Cole has already composed his first song, a multi-part piano piece dedicated to his mother, entitled *Song of the Birds*. He shows almost the precocity of a young Mozart, which becomes even more striking at age 14, when Kate falsifies his school records to subtract a year from his birth age, making him appear even more of a child prodigy. She also uses family money to subsidize school orchestral performances, where Cole is given starring violin roles, and to influence the billing and reporting of the concerts in the local press. Cole wealth and cachet goes far in Peru.

What it can't buy the young Cole, however, is popularity. This is Peru, Indiana, after all; such a proverbial hicksville that Groucho Marx, ever worried that his jokes might grow too highbrow, later asked: "What'll it mean to the barber in Peru?" Kate's cosseting of her child shows in the Little Lord Fauntleroy suits she dresses him in, which earn the kind of ridicule that you'd expect from kids anywhere, but above all, in Peru, Ind. Predictably, young Cole grows up shy, and lonely.

In 1905, J.O. packs Cole off east to the Worcester Academy, Massachusetts; one of the country's oldest and most prestigious private schools. Packs, literally, for thanks to the family money, Cole is able to bring an upright piano with him in his baggage train. The piano and Cole's musical gifts become his keys to social success, and this early linkage of musicianship with popularity and social facility plays an important part in his development. So does the dean of the college, Dr. Daniel W. Abercrombie, who becomes an influence guide in his music teaching. "Words and music must be so inseparably wedded to each other that they are like one," runs one of Dr. Abercrombie's maxims, and Cole takes it to heart. At Worcester, he prospers, and apparently prefers life among the hills and maples of New England to the flat farmlands of Indiana, rarely returning home. He also makes his first exploratory flirtations with girls in his senior year, before his preference for men grows fully evident. He becomes class valedictorian, and J.O. rewards him with a European tour, through France, Switzerland and Germany.

Cole graduates from Worcester to Yale in 1909, majoring in English with a minor in music. Some Yale men initially receive him as a gauche Westerner ill-suited to the Ivy League milieu, affecting eccentricities such as salmon-coloured ties and manicured nails, but he soon outgrows that categorization, and wins his way into the hearts of his new peers with his wit and his gift of song. He writes fight songs for the Yale Bulldogs, and musical comedies for the Yale Dramatic Association, periodically appearing onstage in drag. His wit earns him a contributor's slot at *The Yale Record*, now the world's oldest humour magazine. He becomes a frat boy with the Delta Kappa Epsilon fraternity, and pens mini-revues for his frat brothers. He joins the newly-formed Yale Whiffenpoofs, America's oldest collegiate *a cappella* singing group. In his senior year, he is inducted into the Scroll and Key Society, and in the same year, is elected President of the Yale Glee Club, touring the nation in a triumphal progress that wins him standing ovations for his original songs, and the promise of a national audience beyond the courts and cloisters of Yale.

By the time he graduates from Yale in 1913, Cole has over 300 songs and musical works under his belt, including six full-scale musical comedies. He's already used New Haven as a springboard to Manhattan and New York nightlife, taking the train to town with classmates for dinner and a show, before returning to Yale the next morning. On one of these jaunts, he meets Ada "Bricktop'" Smith at a cabaret and learns the Charleston from her. Broadway beckons.

J.O., however, tries to steer his wayward grandson into a more serious career, and shepherds him into Harvard Law School. Cole proves not cut out for the bar. He neglects his studies, and according to one apocryphal tale, is pressed one day by the professor after failing to revise a case, "Mr. Porter, why don't you learn to play the fiddle?" Cole can take a hint, especially such an apposite one. He gets up and leaves the class, never to return. He doesn't go far, though. Instead, at the suggestion of the dean of the Law School, he transfers to Harvard School of Music in his second year, where he studies under Pietro Yon. His mother withholds the news from J.O. for the time being.

In 1915, Cole abandons Harvard for the Yale Club on Vanderbilt Avenue, and sells his first song for a Broadway show, "Esmeralda," for the revue *Hands Up*. That first debut is premature. His own first Broadway show, *See America First*, a spoof patriotic mish-mash with a few songs from his Yale years, opens at the Maxine Elliott Theatre in March 1916, after a reasonably successful provincial run. Its financiers include Anne Morgan, daughter of J. P. Morgan, and influential interior designer Elsie de Wolfe. But high society support isn't enough for Broadway, and the show closes after only 15 performances. "A high-class college show played partly by professionals," the *New York American* dubs it. Mortified, Cole floats no more productions before leaving for Paris in July 1917, following the entry of the United States into World War I.

Cole later fosters the legend that he joined the French Foreign Legion in France, and taught gunnery to American soldiers near Paris. In fact, he joins the Duryea Relief organization, visiting towns devastated by the Germans. His off-duty existence in Paris, though, is every bit as romantic as the legend, and his luxury apartment becomes the locus for wild decadent parties, with every kind of contemporary vice, especially the sexually ambiguous kind. The War to End All Wars ends, but Cole goes on living in Paris, taking composition classes amid the social whirl. According to contemporary accounts, he spends his mornings writing songs, before lunchtime champagne cocktails at the Ritz and naps in the afternoon.

Unexpectedly, the Parisian high life proves Cole's salvation. At the Ritz, at a society wedding in January 1918, he meets Linda Lee Thomas, a divorced Virginia socialite eight years his senior. They grow closer and closer, and in December 1919, they marry in the 18th arrondissement. For all his homosexuality, the union proves a long and happy one. Linda even conceives later, though she miscarries. She provides the firm maternal guidance he has grown accustomed to, and pushes him to more serious work and study.

In 1919, Cole also has his first Broadway success, dishing up the music and lyrics for the third *Hitchy-Koo* revue, which runs for 56 performances. He follows this in 1920 with numbers for the musical *A Night Out*, a West End theatre success in London. Linda persuades Cole to enrol that year at the Schola Cantorum de Paris, where he studies under Vincent d'Indy, although he can only bear the academic strictures for a few months. A smattering of commissions for songs and numbers follow over the next few years.

Despite the trickle of work, Cole has come into his own in more ways than one. That same year, J.O. dies at the grand old age of 94. Kate gives her son half of her inheritance, and Cole is literally worth a million dollars. The few external restraints on his extravagant tastes are removed. The palatial Porter home in the rue Monsieur is decked out in platinum wallpaper and zebra-skin upholstery. Bricktop is a regular guest and performer at his soirees. Cole rents a series of Venetian palazzi as summer retreats, at an average $4,000 per month, and hires the entire Ballets Russes for his parties, although Sergei Diaghilev's secretary Boris Kochno, ungratefully complains that all Venice is up in arms against Cole because of his jazz and his multiracial guests. The train journeys from Paris to Venice are epics in themselves, occupying eight or nine compartments: one for Cole, one for his wife, two for a maid and a valet, a fifth full of laundry facilities to steam and press the Porter wardrobe, a sixth as an impromptu bar, and the rest for friends along for the ride.

Cole is not just a profligate and playboy, however; he is also a knowledgeable and diligent craftsman. He may not have been the most consistent and thorough of students, but he already has far more formal musical training and understanding than almost any of his songwriter contemporaries. Cole, some will claim later, is pioneering the displacement of classical music by popular music as the defining cultural form of his society, by taking the classical disciplines and applying them to popular songs. He's also at the forefront of the displacement of the old triple-time rhythms of European music, from ballads to the waltz, by the four/four double-time beat of black African tradition, freely moving between both. And he knows very well what he's doing. He delivers complete scores to his publishers, unlike the rudimentary sketches of other songsmiths of the day, and checks the proofs painstakingly before printing. By 1923 he has already written a short ballet, *Within the Quota*, performed by the Ballets Suédois, then at its height as a synthesis of the avant-garde in all the arts, which opens on the same night as Milhaud's *La création du monde*. He also writes most of the numbers for the 1924 season of the *Greenwich Village Follies*, but by the end of its Broadway run, most of his contributions have been dropped, and the disappointment almost drives him to give up public songwriting altogether. He certainly doesn't need the money, after all. Sheer love of his craft keeps him going.

A few years later, though, Cole unexpectedly has his first Broadway hit. In 1928, Broadway producer E. Ray Goetz commissions him to write the songs for the musical *Paris*. The star, Irène Bordoni, originally wanted Rodgers and Hart, but they were unavailable, and Porter's agent persuades Goetz to engage Cole instead. They all convince Cole to give Broadway another try. While he is working on the musical, his father dies in August 1928, and Cole takes a brief furlough in Indiana before returning to work. When the show opens on Broadway in October 1928 at the Music Box Theater, after the usual provincial try-out, it includes "Let's Fall In Love," an instant hit. Cole misses the opening night because he's in the real Paris, supervising the opening of another show, *La Revue*, which also proves a success, doing his international reputation no harm at all. *Paris* runs for 195 performances, and in 1929 Warner Brothers turns it into a movie.

Cole now has definite star quality. English producer C.B. Cochran decides to cash in on this rising fame, and commissions Cole to write the songs for a musical revue called *Wake Up and Dream*. "Let's Fall in Love" is included in the

London run, but Cole pens "What Is This Thing Called Love?" for the show, creating another immediate hit. *Wake Up and Dream* runs for 263 shows in London, before opening on Broadway on 30 December 1929, soon after the Wall Street Crash, making it the last Broadway show of the Twenties. While *Wake Up and Dream* is still enjoying its London success, Cole has penned another show, *Fifty Million Frenchmen*, which opens on Broadway on 27 November, directed by old Yale chum Monty Woolley and produced by Goetz. It contains another instant classic, "You Do Something to Me," doing that voodoo to audiences that Cole's fans grow to know so well. The Depression cuts *Wake Up and Dream*'s Broadway run to only 136 performances, but *Fifty Million Frenchmen* runs for 254, after an adulatory notice from Irving Berlin, who calls it "the best musical comedy I have seen in years."

The Crash ruins one Broadway producer after another, but Cole Porter has proved able to keep shows in business, Depression or no. Goetz offers Cole and Woolley another project, *The New Yorkers*, envisaged as a vehicle for Jimmy "the Schnozzle" Durante, already a vaudeville star. Durante writes 5 of the show's 17 songs, but Cole's contribution includes yet another hit, "I Happen to Like New York," as well as a *succès de scandale*, "Love For Sale." *The New Yorkers* opens at the Broadway Theatre on 8 December 1930, and runs for 168 performances.

Cole consolidates his conquest of the New York musical scene with *Gay Divorce*, Fred Astaire's last Broadway musical. In the show, Astaire debuts "Night and Day," almost Cole's signature number, inspired, according to some accounts, by a call to prayer that Cole heard in Morocco. With that song, and Astaire, the show runs for 248 performances after its Broadway debut on 29 November 1932. Cole delivers another London production the following year, *Nymph Errant,* deemed too English for audiences Stateside. It's *Anything Goes* in 1934, though, that truly establishes his ascendancy. Cole is the lyricist for a book conceived by producer Vinton Freedley and penned by P. G. Wodehouse and Guy Bolton, starring Ethel Merman.

At the height of his powers, Cole produces what he later dubs one of his perfect shows. The feature numbers include "Anything Goes", "You're the Top", and "I Get a Kick Out of You." The plot, such as it is, concerns high jinks at sea. Just before the show's opening, a disastrous fire aboard the liner SS *Morro Castle* – incidentally the trigger for some major revisions in maritime safety practices – forces a last-minute revision of the plot. All the same, from its opening on 21 November 1934 at the Alvin Theater Broadway, the show is a triumph, running for 420 performances.

Buoyed by the success of *Anything Goes,* Cole and his collaborator Moss Hart decide in 1935 to take a world cruise with families and friends, and turn the experience into a musical. The ship they select is the RMS *Franconia.*

That same year, at Broadway's Imperial Theatre, a rising young clarinetist is attracting attention in a swing concert with his "Interlude in B-flat." His name is Artie Shaw.

Chapter 5

Artie Shaw is a New Yorker by birth, with just the kind of mixed pedigree that often comes as part of the deal. He is born Arthur Jacob Arshawsky on 23 May 1910, almost concurrently with John Graham, to a Jewish father ostensibly from Russia and an Austrian Jewish mother, who run a dressmaking business in the Lower East Side, while his father also moonlights as a portrait photographer. His father has other side interests: he's a frustrated musician and inventor, whose real place of origin was probably Odessa. Artie has the kind of metropolitan origins that Cole Porter, the hick from Peru, later aspires to; he just isn't so lucky in his status. Nor in his family's commercial gifts: in 1918, the family business goes bankrupt, and they have to leave New York.

At age seven, Artie moves with his family to York Street in New Haven, Connecticut, where they resume the dressmaking business. New Haven, where Cole Porter had such a high old time at Yale, isn't so welcoming for a poor Jewish boy with an obvious, and preposterous, name. At least New Haven helps build his respect for learning. In later life, he recalls the shadow cast over New Haven by Yale. Artie is already a somewhat shy, thoughtful, imaginative kid, an avid reader of Robert Louis Stevenson and Mark Twain. Such niceties are lost on his fellow pupils at Dwight Street School, who only pick up on one thing. "We don't want no goddamn Christ-killers saying the Lord's Prayer around here. Keep your dirty sheeny nose out of other people's prayers," they taunt him. Artie becomes a troubled, and troublesome, child, victim, in his own estimation of terrible anti-Semitism. With a BB gun, he unwittingly shoots into a nearby classroom; the police call next day to take the gun away. Artie's father takes out his anger by stamping his son's model planes underfoot.

New Haven, heart of WASP supremacy, doesn't look like it's going to have anything to offer young Artie. "In those days, you had to be a Gentile in America to work," he says later.

Unexpectedly, music comes to the rescue. His mother decides that piano lessons might cure his son's ills, and obtains a piano and a course of lessons. As the violin to Cole, so the piano to Artie: both resent the first instruments and lessons their mothers thrust on them. Artie pushes back against the piano lessons his mother foists on him, but learns to love the ukulele, and plays hooky to spend time at the local vaudeville house, Poli's Palace Theatre, on Church Street. There, one day, he sees a saxophone player who impresses the hell out of him. The 13-year-old Artie gets a job as an errand boy for the local delicatessen, and works until he's saved up enough to buy his own sax. Once he has it, he practises eight hours a day until his lips bleed. As the piano to Cole, so the sax to Artie: the key for the introverted only child to open the door and reach out to others. His father is less receptive. Always ready to crush others' aspirations as his own were crushed, he dismisses his son's new pride and joy as a "blosser" – Yiddish for a kazoo.

Consumed by his bitterness and disappointments, Artie's father deserts his family and moves to California. He promises to call his family to join him later, but never follows through. Left with his mother, Artie moves on to an alto sax, then forms a small band with friends, the Peter Pan Novelty Orchestra. In 1924, aged 15, he drops out of school and changes his name to Shaw, aping the lost inheritance of the hero of *Kidnapped*. He puts the name change down to shame at his Jewish roots, but he soon discovers that, in the world of popular music, of Benny Goodman and Irving Aaronson, Roger Wolfe Kahn and Irving Berlin, Jewish roots are not such a handicap as in regular American society. He joins the dance band of local bandleader Johnny Cavallaro as alto saxophonist. Cavallaro soon fires him, over a misunderstanding involving Artie's first encounter with alcohol and his appearance onstage clad only in his bathing trunks, then re-engages him, demanding this time that he learn the clarinet. Artie's fine with this. "I was learning music," he says later. "I'm not interested in the instrument. The instrument is a means." Cavallaro decides that the results aren't worth keeping, though, and fires him again.

Artie gets a job at the Olympia movie theatre in New Haven, studying his craft and perfecting his sight reading. Overworked at the Olympia, he lands a new job in a Chinese restaurant band in Cleveland, Ohio. His bandmates notice that he has a habit of listening to classical records, then reinterpreting the music on his clarinet: they nickname him "Little Beethoven." In Cleveland, Artie has a chance to hear great black jazz musicians: Coleman Hawkins, Art Tatum. He also runs across a stack of Louis Armstrong records, and experiences a revelation: "It was like instant satori. I couldn't believe what I heard. It was 'dirty' music; meaning, he'd slur notes, do things that a trained musician was taught not to do. And yet it all worked." Artie takes a week off and drives from Cleveland to Chicago to hear Armstrong play at the Savoy.

In 1929, Artie wins an Ohio essay and songwriting competition, and with the prize, an expenses-paid trip to Hollywood, revisits his father. He also meets up with members of Irving Aaronson's Commanders, and after six months back in Cleveland, moves to Hollywood to join the band – just after its appearance in Cole Porter's *Paris* and hit recording of Cole's "Let's Misbehave." Aaronson's touring schedule includes a six-week gig at the Granada Café in Chicago in the summer of 1930, where Artie meets Benny Goodman, Bix Beiderbecke, Bud Freeman, Earl Hines and other jazz luminaries. He makes a good impression in person: tall, dark-haired, suave. His new persona gives him the confidence, even brashness, that Arshawsky could have never had. The metropolitan environment of Chicago also gives Artie the chance to make a serious acquaintance with modern classical music – Stravinsky, Debussy, Bartok and Ravel. He claims later to have listened to "La Mer" a hundred times. In the late summer, he receives news that his father is seriously ill in California; when a telegram announcing his father's death arrives, Artie breaks into hysterical laughter.

When Irving Aaronson's Commanders finally reaches New York, Artie catches another break – not a good one. On the morning of 15 October 1930, his car hits and kills a 60-year-old yacht chef, George Woods, crossing the street at Broadway and 91st. The subsequent police investigation clears Artie of any criminal wrongdoing, but the dead man's family files a civil suit against him for damages of $80,000. Artie has to stay in New York for the court proceedings, parting company with Irving Aaronson's Commanders, and union rules prevent him taking new work in the city until he has been in residence long enough to get his 802 card. Impoverished, he takes to wandering the wintry streets of the city alone, finally finding his way to Harlem and Pod's and Jerry's (officially the Catagonia Club), to hear house pianist Willie "The Lion" Smith play. The two strike up a musical brotherhood, and Smith becomes a guide and mentor. It surely doesn't hurt that Smith is the son of a Jewish father, though he hides it well. Artie finally frees himself of his legal entanglements only by declaring bankruptcy. In the spring of 1931 he gets his union card, and by August is playing in the CBS radio orchestra. At age 21, he is the leading New York session player for studio and radio work in alto sax and clarinet. He elopes with a 17-year-old doctor's daughter, Jane Cairns, an old Ohio acquaintance, but her father has the marriage annulled.

In 1932, CBS cut their staff and Artie joins the orchestra of a similarly gifted Jewish contemporary, Roger Wolfe Kahn, and makes a few recordings of current jazz hits. When Kahn has his band filmed playing on board a yacht, Artie is the star, centre stage, in blazer and sailor's cap, delivering a searing clarinet solo. Kahn winds up his band, though, to pursue his other interest of aviation, and Artie is left at a loss again. He is soon remarried, to Margaret Allen, a dental nurse. Always a voracious reader, he also displays the same commitment to literature he has had since a boy, and decides to quit the music business to retire to a small property he's bought in Bucks County, Pennsylvania, 27 acres of land with a house and a broken-down barn, and write a biography of his dead idol Bix Beiderbecke. While chopping wood there, he almost cuts off his left index finger; Margaret employs her professional skills and reattaches it. By 1934 he has given up on writing and country life, and is back in New York. By 1935 he is attracting attention for unusual instrumentation in his ensembles, including some concerts backed only by a rhythm section and a string quartet. Session work pays the rent, but Artie chafes at the endless commercial drivel he is forced to churn out. He is also reading as omnivorously as ever, and auditing classes at Columbia and New York University, eager to pick up on the studies he forsook in his mid-teens. A stock picture of him in 1935 shows Artie almost supernaturally suave in white tie and tails, hair slicked back, breast pocket handkerchief precisely folded. All the discipline and dedication he puts into perfecting his musicianship are on show in his public persona. A handsome guy who, as his friends point out, doesn't look Jewish, he's internalized the contemporary Leslie Howard Clark Gable goy ideal of the Saxon idol. With all that talent and charisma, it's as though he is waiting for his moment, to rise from highly-regarded professional and come into his own.

Chapter 6

It's early January 1935 when Cole Porter and his party set out on their five-month odyssey aboard the RMS *Franconia*. Complaining that he hates working through the cold winter months, Moss Hart proposes Morocco as the venue for their long-awaited collaboration. Cole goes one better, and suggests a world cruise with Cunard, which offers an advertised "38,000 miles of continuous sunshine across the southern hemisphere." Their entourage includes Linda, their servants, and Cole's close friends and fellow gay Yale men Monty Woolley and Howard Sturges. Their goal is to return to New York in the spring with a completed musical ready for production.

Despite the workmanlike purpose of the cruise, and the deadlines hanging over their heads, they can put aside everyday cares for a while and pretend they are adventurers or explorers, setting out to behold the world's mysteries and wonders, trunks stowed, suits hung in cabin wardrobes, shirts and ties and handkerchiefs laid out in chests of drawers, installed in their globetrotting gypsy caravans-with-a-view for a few enchanting months, with a cavalcade of the world's most magnificent monuments and exotic locations paraded past their portholes as though drilled and displayed for their personal amusement. It's an entertainment that in the 1930s is already sliding down-market into the eagerly waiting hands of the middle classes, but the *Franconia* is designed, and priced, to sustain that air of exclusivity for the cosmopolitan elite, with 144 days ahead afloat in the company of the beau monde, a free-floating island of self-styled refinement.

By this time, John has grown used to the routine of warm-weather cruises. Separated from the *Franconia*'s glamorous clientele by the rigid social distinctions of an English ship and the functional divisions of deck crew versus stewards, he has come to think of the passengers as cargo, or at best, steerage; simply items to be stowed away and conveyed from place to place. That distinction only breaks down when he's called to take charge of the tenders usually slung on the boat deck davits, and ferry parties ashore, or oversee the local port's arrangements for same. From a mariner's perspective, there's a certain pointlessness to these journeys to nowhere, following the same itinerary only to end up where they started from; so much less purposeful than a definite course from A to B with a set objective. Still, it's a living, on shipboard, and John loves the *Franconia*, for its engineering rather than its decor. With a true mariner, a voyage is not about the destination; it's about the smooth working of the ship en route, the satisfaction of a good passage or the challenges met along the way. So, when John learns that he will be helping to convey the party of Cole Porter, the celebrated Broadway songwriter, the news awakens only passing interest in him. Some of the *Franconia*'s stuffier officers and ratings might complain about the Yankee tunesmith whose latest hit praises that seditious Indian Mahatma Gandhi, but John has never been an especially political animal.

The ship sets sail from New York on 11 January 1935. Cole's baggage includes a small piano-organ, a typewriter, a personal phonograph with discs, a metronome and cases of champagne. "We are all a little dazed," he writes on 14 January to Clifton Webb. "The boat is a joy. There never *was* such balmy weather, and our little gang has been so happy together."

Moss Hart has been fretting that Cole will just indulge himself *en voyage* and deliver no work at all; he needn't have worried. Cole gets into his rhythm early in the cruise. He breakfasts on deck, then visits the barber, then works on deck from morning till noon in his bathing suit, occasionally pausing for a dip, then lunch at one, followed by a nap, and a further two hours' work before a session in the gym, dinner, shipboard diversions such as dancing or cards, and bed by ten.

Cole's inspiration sparks at their very first port of call: the Crown Colony of Jamaica. As a Cunard ship, the *Franconia* has a very English air; even the dinner menus include the likes of mint sauce and Aylesbury duckling between the more exalted heights of *haute cuisine*. Her itineraries are inevitably predisposed towards His Majesty's Imperial possessions, and

Kingston is a natural first stop. Strolling in the Royal Botanical Garden, Cole spies a noisy yellow-eyed bird in a tree and asks what it is. He is told "a kling-kling bird on a divi-divi tree." Immediately, he has the germ of his first song for the upcoming musical, a parody of Noel Coward's lyric style. (The great-tailed grackle is also native to the southern US, and often referred to there simply as a blackbird, but Cole is no ornithologist.)

After passage through the Panama Canal, the *Franconia* docks in Los Angeles on 26 January. A predictable routine of parties and get-togethers follows. Cole and his entourage enjoy a wild evening in Bel-Air thrown by Samuel Goldwyn, with the Marx Brothers and Charles Chaplin in attendance, and meet up with Jerome Kern, Oscar Hammerstein and Irving Berlin. Cunard has just introduced a new staff position of Spiritual Director on board its ships, with a New York Episcopalian and a Detroit Monsignor assigned to this voyage, but Cole makes little use of their services.

From LA it's on to Hilo, then Tahiti. A typhoon bars landfall on Gauguin's island, so instead the ship heads south to Pago Pago in American Samoa. At Fiji, John takes a boat party out to bring the uncrowned King of Fiji aboard as a guest, for an evening screening of Disney's *Three Little Pigs*. It's a formal affair, with due protocol, a well-polished launch, and all uniforms starched and brilliantly clean. The King keeps his ancestral title, even though neither the British colonial government nor the paramount chiefs recognize it, and the titular monarch of the Crown Colony of Fiji is the British Crown. After this, the stops in New Zealand and Australia are comparatively drab affairs. At least by the time they make Port Moresby, the first act of the work in progress is done.

Now they're back in tropic waters again, north of Capricorn, cruising westward from New Guinea through the Torres Strait and the Arafura Sea, past Thursday Island and Darwin, to the Lesser Sunda Islands. The *Franconia* is built for these waters, her freshly repainted white superstructure shining above the waves, but John is a little concerned now about her air conditioning system – one of her greatest innovations and selling points when she was first laid down, and doubly essential now. There are concerns about the health and safety of passengers sleeping directly in the air currents from the ventilators and electric fans, and a warning has already been published in the *Franconia*'s onboard "Cruise News" bulletin. John decides to inspect the entire system. One of the below-decks crew takes him on a tour of the system of conduits, stopping off at the cold room, where icy tigers, leopards, swans, argosies and other table centrepieces sleep in the darkness amid great blocks of ice, like the Snow Queen's menagerie.

"We once had a dead man in here," the engineer explains. "One of the waiters in First Class. He was busy serving cocktails in the smoking room and he dropped dead on the spot. Some kind of syncope, the doctor said. Well, we told the passengers he'd just fainted, and carried him out. Doctor examined him and said he was a dead 'un. We were mid-Atlantic, so what could we do? *Franconia*, she ain't got no refrigerators, just the cold store, so, we put him in cold storage till we reached Rio, laid him out on top of the ice blocks. He was stiff as a board when we carried him out. Had to fold him up something horrible to get him in the stores lift."

Their first port of call in the Dutch East Indies is Kalabahi, capital of Alor Island, just north of the divided island of Timor. Thirties Kalabahi is the kind of place tagged in contemporary newsreels as "a primitive little port" outside recorded history, populated by "some of the strangest-looking human creatures on the earth… weird caricatures of human life," a cliche for "a primitive land of fear," untouched by civilization. A more sympathetic eye might have noted an indigenous Melanesian population with a considerable admixture of Javanese settlers and traditions. That said, the same newsreels do play tribute to "the important part that dancing plays in the lives of primitive people," and it's this musical tradition of drums and gongs – for Alor perpetuates the legacies of the great Indonesian culture centres further west – that will deliver inspiration to Cole.

Act II of Cole's work in progress begins with the landing in

Kalabahi. The small port, hardly more than a village, is at the eastern end of a deep inlet, with no wharf for a liner like the *Franconia* to moor at. She rides at anchor out in the bay, framed by the deep green of the mountains, while John oversees the launches ferrying the landing party and passengers ashore, the crew dressed for the occasion in blazing white linens and solar topees, incongruous against a background of bronzed bodies and chequered sarongs. The crew bring a table ashore, and distribute cheese and fruit, preserves and pearl shells, as payment for the entertainment. Then Cole and his party settle under the waving palms to watch the dance and hear the music.

   Cole and his party are entertained with a local dance. It's his first encounter with Indonesian music, and the melody inspires him. The first few bars of the music he heard becomes the germ of something new. Back on board, Cole shuts himself away in his cabin to work unceasingly until he has licked the new composition into shape. In Bali, where they are treated to more classical Balinese dance, the experience is reinforced, by dancers and musicians who stun Cole with their sheer beauty. Balinese music has confirmed his love of semitones and minor keys, their dark complexity and bitter-sweet zest. It also has reinforced the value of shifting tempi and keys. Yet he draws the rhythm from a different place, from the recollection of a Martiniquais traditional dance he saw in a Left Bank nightclub during his Paris years, a dance called the Beguine. At the time, the rumba-like rhythm of the dance impressed him, and he noted down "Begin the Beguine" as a likely title for a song. It's been waiting in his notes for a decade. By the time he has the tune close to its final form, it extends over 108 bars, never quite repeating itself, far from the typical AABA structure of contemporary songs, African and Asian influences fusing inextricably in the crucible of a true creative spirit that blends and melds the most disparate materials into one whole. The notes tinkle out of his cabin portholes, out through his cabin door, and drift between decks, reaching the ears of the crew, including John.

Then the ship turns north, for the rather more pedestrian passage of the Straits of Malacca and the Bay of Bengal, from Singapore to Penang, thence to Madras and Colombo. No question here that the *Franconia* is in British waters, with the magic of Bali left far behind. At every port, a Government House; along every waterfront, white plasterwork and bustling docks. The ship's orchestra has developed a bad habit of breaking into "You're the Top" or "I Get a Kick Out of You" every time the Porter party enters the ship's lounge or dining salon. Monty Woolley and Howard Sturges have taken to groaning loudly whenever they hear the first bars. The party studiously avoids the "Franconia Follies" amateur dramatics on the boat deck, presented by their fellow passengers.

John has little to see to in these waters, with the highly professional pilotage and local boat services at every stop, but he busies himself plotting out the tideways and anchorages, calculating how best to handle debarkation and loading if he was called to run one of the launches out. He also prefers to avoid the snobbish atmosphere of British colonies, and especially the Raj, where social distinctions are minutely reinforced and junior officers are disdained. Despite the long palm-fringed beaches along the shores, and the mosques and gopurams outlined against majestic sunsets, he feels somehow that he has left romance behind on the far side of the Java Sea, and it's only once the *Franconia* is far out in the Indian Ocean, bound for Port Victoria and the Seychelles, that he feels that elusive sensation stealing back over him.

The Seychelles, according to the newsreels, are traditionally associated with "the original garden of Eden." The sheer natural beauty of the islands for once matches that tinge of touristic hyperbole, with a population then hovering around 30,000 living along the palm-shaded shores, enjoying what the newsreels describe as "a civilization of their own," that has been by and large appropriated for the cultivation of copra. While the Porter party are being entertained at Government House, whose long white verandahs look down on Victoria Pier from the direction of Bel Air, John joins a group of fellow officers invited to a tea dance hosted by the local planters' club. The officers are politely, apologetically informed that they would have been received at Government House as well, but for the Cunard restrictions on passengers fraternizing with crew. Instead, they are entertained at the Judge's House, a former wing of the old Government House which still retains some of its former dignity.

On the rickshaw ride from the Pier, John sees few of the "natural, carefree and happy people, resorting to childlike celebrations at the slightest provocation" that the newsreels promise in Victoria, with its two main streets meeting at the central clock tower, and the spider's web of of cart tracks, bridle paths, lanes and footpaths surrounding them, where rickshaws whisk passengers to and fro. The ship is just visible over the rooftops, exactly like Cunard's promotional pictures of the period, with the *Franconia* off in the bay, glittering above the sloping tin roofs of the houses. The people are mostly East African creoles, with a scattering of Arabs, Chinese and Indians. There is an air of stultifying stagnation about the place, linked to the Depression-era price of copra. Houses and shops are low, timber-built affairs with corrugated iron roofs, though a few are distinguished by walls of limestone coral. A couple of John's shipmates have disappeared into those warrens in search of less refined amusements: John lost his virginity on one such outing in Halifax, and that experience reduced his appetite for similar forays in future. It wasn't the act itself, or the considerate, attentive French girl who ministered to him, that put him off, so much as the brutality of his fellow seamen in bundling him into the house and berating the whores afterwards.

There's nothing like that this time. The convoy of rickshaws rattles and clatters the short distance to the Judge's House, a white-boarded building with shutters and double peaked roofs, where a delegation of the better sort of islanders are waiting to receive them. The reception rooms have been decorated with garlands of flowers, and supplied with trestles holding tea urns and glass jugs of chastely non-alcoholic refreshments under the revolving ceiling fans. There's a very small orchestra, more of a band really, on a separate dais, all of them black, playing the likes of "Tea for Two," "Sometimes I'm Happy," and "On the Sunny Side of the Street," very strictly, formally and quietly.

  A few of the local plantocracy and their wives are there to make conversation, much of it with a French accent, and stand up for the honour of the island. A gaggle of decorous, white-dressed girls in their teens, evidently the daughters of the better island families, are gathered in one corner under the watchful eye of a chaperone. Clearly, the local gentry want their girls to pick up a smattering of cosmopolitan culture and savoir-faire from acquaintance with the officer class, without any indecorous attachments. The French origins of the colony are obvious in the sprinkling of octoroon and Creole complexions among them, the accents and occasional dips into rapid, giggling French, and something indefinable in their carriage and embonpoint, so different from an English girl on such an occasion.

  One girl especially stands out: she's as dark-haired as any of her companions, but her complexion is clearer, and her bone structure sharper; she could easily pass for a Spaniard or even a Parisienne. John thinks back to the Ceylonese girls he saw in Colombo, but her skin is paler, though her eyes are just as dark and full. She catches sight of him gazing at her, and flashes him a smile as bright as any Creole. He colours, and hopes that his flush won't show above his collar. All the same, he's conscious that he must cut quite a figure himself in his immaculate white uniform. Tea dances are practically a Royal Navy tradition, and John's smattering of Senior Service experience has left him familiar with their etiquette. He goes up to her and offers her his arm.

  "Excuse me, Miss, I hope I'm not disturbing you, but might I offer you a coconut cup?" he asks.

  She lowers her head shyly, but accepts his arm and lets him lead her away from her giggling fellows. The chaperone's sharp eye is on them, and John is careful to be on his best behaviour.

  "I'm John Graham, Junior Third Officer from the *Franconia*," he introduces himself.

"Farah Ayad; from Victoria Etoile School, not anything," she responds, with a sardonic twitch to her lip. Her accent is decidedly less French than the others he has heard, almost more clearly English than his own.

John leads her to the side table where another immaculately clad black steward is ladling out some innocuous coconut concoction, and takes her glass for her, then escorts her to a rattan table beside the small and still empty dance floor. With her white dress, white stockings, glass of white punch, against the white drapes and plasterwork, and him by her side in his white uniform, she's quite the composition in white.

"Farah is a lovely name," he remarks, thinking to bolster her self-esteem. "I hope you don't mind me saying that it doesn't sound very French, though."

"Oh, it's not." She takes a short sip of the coconut, leaving a little white on her dark lips. "Papa is Arab, you see. He's a doctor. We pray at the Victoria Mosque. He's very free-thinking though; admires the Turks, always talking about laic things, and he sent me to a local Catholic school. He believes they take better care of the girls' achievements and their virtue there."

She ducks her head in a coy, knowing way. Surely this little chit of a girl can't be so sophisticated? John wonders if some trick has been played on him.

"So you're not from here?" he asks.

"Oh no; Mama is from Ceylon and I was born there. Papa brought us here because he thought there would be more opportunities and fewer doctors on the island. I suppose he was right. He treats most of the planters, and sends me to school with their daughters. They don't appear to care that much that I'm a Muslim. I suppose it's part of the French way."

John certainly is struggling to fit this composed young miss in her white muslin dress to his past impressions of heavily covered figures seen dimly on the street in Zanzibar or Aden. The dance orchestra limps into Noël Coward's "World Weary." One or two couples have taken to the floor for a few experimental circuits by this time, and John feels able to ask Farah to dance without exposing her to too much scrutiny. He is aware that the chaperone will step in if he holds her too close, so he keeps a modest separation between them, despite the allure of her full breasts under the white dress, and somehow they manage to follow the steps of the dance.

"So, I hear that your ship has all sorts of famous people on board," she looks up at him, fluttering her dark eyelashes. "Is there anyone I'd know?"

John struggles to think. "Well, we're carrying Cole Porter on this trip; the famous Broadway composer. Do you know him?"

She lifts her eyebrows in surprise. "Oh, the one who wrote 'You Do Something to Me?' Yes, I do know him, though I think that's the only song by him that I can remember. We don't get many of the latest tunes all the way out here, I'm afraid," she sighs.

"Well, I think I can tell you his latest," he boasts, and begins to whistle what he can remember from the tune he heard floating out of Cole Porter's cabin.

Farah cocks an ear, listens hard, smiles, then giggles, more and more uncontrollably. Finally, almost doubled over, she lets him lead her back to their seats. The chaperone on the other side of the room looks scandalized, but it's obvious that her charge is extremely amused, rather than shocked.

"I'm sorry, Mr Graham, but you're no whistler. Please, I really am sorry; not everyone can be good at everything."

John tries to regain his composure. Just then, the band breaks into Porter's "You're the Top." They look at each other, and both burst out laughing again.

"Well, your English is really very good," he compliments her, anxious to get the conversation onto a different track and settle things down again before the chaperone intervenes.

"Much good it may do me," she sighs. "I want to get off the island, study, see more of the world. If I got an independent Seychelles scholarship, I could go to study in Great Britain. Father wants me to study somewhere closer to home: however much of a freethinker he is, he does want to protect his only daughter. But I'm sure that Britain is better, don't you think?"

John stops, actually embarrassed. "I wouldn't know too well: I'm not a university boy, I'm afraid," he flusters. "I had all my education at sea. I do know that the University in Glasgow was one of the first to admit girls as full students. I come from there, you see."

Farah lifts an eyebrow. "Oh? That's interesting. Perhaps I'll apply there then."

"And what would you study if you could?" he asks, intrigued.

"Oh, economics. I love figures. Mummy says I'd make an excellent storekeeper," she giggles.

Acting on a sudden impulse, he whispers: "I could help you, you know. If you like. Not with the maths; I mean making your applications and all that."

"Oh, could you?" she beams. "That would be most frightfully decent of you. But please don't feel obliged."

"No, it'd be an honour, please," he persists, though in fact he has no idea at all what he's doing. "My family lives there, after all. I'm sure they'd be glad to help."

"Hmm." She frowns, and for a moment, John fears he's gone too far. "I can't write my address down for you now; Mme Vallotton will think it's for some silly assignation. I know: write to me at the Doctor's House on rue Royale. Everyone knows my father. Just put that and my name, and the note will be sure to get there."

"I will." In the background, the chaperone is making the chivvying motions that indicate she has to take her charges away. Farah gets up, with a last shy smile, and he stands to say goodbye.

"Well, thank you, Officer Graham," she says in a low voice. A brief, smooth, cool clasp of her hand, and she is away.

John's conscientious maritime habits ensure that he has a pocketbook and a pencil on his person at all times, and he discreetly notes down Farah's name and address before rejoining his own party. No one else seems to have noticed much of what went on, or so he thinks at first, but in the swaying rickshaw on the way back to the Dock, his companion leans across to him and whispers, "Well, you seem to have made a bit of a conquest there."

"Oh, it was nothing," John demurs. "Just a little friendly banter, that's all."

"Well, be careful of the dark ones," his companion warns. "Don't want to set the natives on the warpath, what?"

On the East African coast, the *Franconia* makes landfall at Zanzibar, where the Sultan, a dedicated Cole Porter fan, has sent his own launch with equerry to ferry the Porter party to the Palace for a royal audience and a phonograph performance of "Let's Do It." Then south to Madagascar, through the Mozambique Channel and round the Cape of Good Hope, to Cape Town in April, where Moss finishes the musical's book, and then the long South Atlantic crossing to Montevideo. Mid-Atlantic, on 5 May, the *Franconia* being a British ship, everybody raises a glass to the Silver Jubilee of His Royal Highness George V – and Cole and Moss's work-in-progress at last has its title. By their arrival in Rio, Cole has completed the score for *Jubilee*, and on their return to New York on 31 May, Cole and Moss have a complete new musical to present to the world.

Chapter 7

Cole and his party dive straight into preparations for their new show after their return, with castings and rehearsals. The plot of *Jubilee* is as flimsy as many a Broadway farce, concerning a fugitive royal family and the various celebrity caricatures they briefly fall in with. There's a solid Broadway ensemble cast, and Monty Woolley helps out with dialogue and direction. The young Montgomery Clift somehow manages to land a bit-part as a prince.

Yet somehow, after all those months at sea, and wave upon wave of inspiration, something doesn't quite jell. After the customary pre-Broadway tryout, *Jubilee* opens on 12 October 1935, at the Imperial Theatre. High society and glitterati are out in force for the opening night – Katherine Hepburn, Tallulah Bankhead, Joan Crawford, Prince Obolensky, Jerome Kern, Elizabeth Arden – in a dress parade of sable and mink. The show has its true standout gems, including "Just One of Those Things" and of course, "Begin the Beguine" – thoroughly oriental in flavour in the show's orchestration, all jungle drums, cymbals and temple gongs. The reviews vary from good to ecstatic. One *Sunday News* reviewer hails it as "the most notable contribution to the American theatre this generation has had a chance to welcome."

All the same, *Jubilee* picks up a reputation for being jinxed. Several fires break out at the theatres in Boston and New York. Mary Bolan, the grande dame of the cast playing the part of the Queen, misses some performances due to drink. Finally, George V, who inspired the title, dies on 20 January 1936. That obviously doesn't help its prospects. Despite the adulatory critical reception, the show closes on 7 May 1936, after only 169 performances, and no theatrical leasing company signs it up for stock or amateur production. This is the kind of result that confirms Cole in his belief that his lyrics are simply too sophisticated for Tin Pan Alley, and that "polished, urbane and adult" writing can never find a lasting home in stage music.

Hollywood is calling, meanwhile, with a contract from MGM,

and Cole and Linda head west in December 1935. The move is no solution to their ills. On the West Coast, Cole becomes more and more flagrantly gay, dressing more brightly and cruising more blatantly. His marriage to Linda was always a delicate balance, and now the Hollywood environment is upsetting it. California is no answer to his creative ills either. He writes the songs for *Born to Dance*, with Eleanor Powell and James Stewart, including "Easy to Love" and "I've Got You Under My Skin," securing a 1936 Academy Award nomination for Best Song, but his next Broadway show, *Red Hot and Blue!* proves a bust. The star Broadway playwriting duo of Lindsay and Crouse have produced a lengthy and bizarre book, including a young girl branded by a waffle iron, and Cole insists on numerous changes, none of which seem to fix it. Even a dream cast of Ethel Merman, Jimmy "the Schnozzle" Durante and the young Bob Hope, even "It's De-Lovely," can't rescue the show. Critics are unappreciative at its opening at the Alvin Theatre on 29 October 1936, and it closes in April 1937 after 183 performances. However mistaken, Cole draws the same conclusion from this setback as he did from the reception of *Jubilee*.

Cole still tries to keep up with the times. In a December 1936 interview with the *New York Herald Tribune*, he reveals: "Recently... I visited a nightclub six times to try to get a feeling of swing in the new tunes played there. I go to the theater constantly to keep in touch with popular musical taste." He claims to follow modern slang and contemporary idioms just as assiduously, to make sure his lyrics are always up to date and with wide appeal.

Back in Hollywood, Cole contributes songs to the 1937 film revival of *Rosalie*, including "In The Still Of The Night." Relations with Linda are still tense, and she is spending more and more of her time at their home in Paris. At this point, she may be considering divorce. Cole travels to Paris to heal the rift, but returns alone in October to New York – and disaster.

On 24 October 1937, Cole suffers an accident at the Piping Rock Club in Nassau County. Piping Rock is a haven for the

New York *crème de la crème*, patronized by Nasts and Doubledays, Astors and Morgans. Cole is out riding with an old friend, the jeweller Duke Fulco di Verdura, when his skittish horse, which he has been warned against, shies and rolls on him, crushing one leg. Attempting to get up, it crushes his other leg. The accident is eerily reminiscent of a similar mishap suffered at the Piping Rock Club by Lida Louise Fleitmann in October 1915.

Cole sustains compound fractures to both femurs, exacerbated by staphylococcal infection of the damaged bones. He has emergency surgery at Glen Cove, then is moved to the Doctors Hospital in Manhattan for the first of many operations to follow. Linda reschedules her transatlantic crossing to be with him. Cole is in and out of consciousness; his doctor advises immediate amputation of both legs. Linda insists on postponement until she arrives, citing the psychological damage such a procedure might cause. By early November, she and his mother are at Cole's side, and all three of them refuse the procedure. Instead, Cole endures an operation to repair damaged leg nerves which leaves him in continual pain. His right leg is covered with blebs, blisters of lymph and other secretions that "look like a flowing mass of lava" when first exposed, and that are as agonizing as burns. Some of these have to be pared away. Cole rechristens his legs: the right, docile Josephine; the left, Geraldine, "a hellion, a bitch, a psychopath." His sedative and painkiller consumption in the hospital peaks at around 14 different kinds of narcotics per day. He describes the sensation as "any number of small, sharply, finely-toothed rakes," scraping up and down his legs. In January he is discharged and returns to his apartment in the Waldorf Towers, but he now depends on braces, sticks and his faithful valet, Paul Sylvain, to carry him around. His right leg remains in a cast.

The Governor of Indiana invites Peru's long-lost son to its first "Cole Porter Day" in spring 1938. Cole declines, pleading ill health, but welcomes "this most extraordinary honor." In his thanks, he writes of "living so long in a world of make-believe, where a kind of transitory tribute is paid one for his so-called good deeds by way of entertainment." In the summer of 1938, he falls in his apartment and breaks his left hip again. His first show after the accident, *You Never Know*, is a flop when it opens on 21 September 1938, but at least it marks his return to creative production. Over the next few years, work will be one of his best escapes from the hell of pain his life has become. Meanwhile, Artie Shaw has taken up the fruit of Cole's cruise, as though the baton has been passed to him, and made it into something new.

Chapter 8

In 1936, aged 26, Artie Shaw forms his first band, and takes it onstage with his own work. The same Imperial Theatre on Broadway that hosted Cole's *Jubilee* has hired him to play a short interlude during a set change in a swing concert. Artie's ensemble consists of a jazz rhythm section, a string quartet and Artie himself on clarinet. A string section is a novelty in a jazz ensemble, and the piece he creates for this new band is "Interlude in B-Flat."

As Cole Porter has brought his classical discipline and technical training into Tin Pan Alley musicals, so Artie Shaw has brought classical influences into the world of jazz. It's part of a new current in contemporary music, midway between both, the so-called Third Stream. His personal technique, however flawless, leads many classically-trained clarinettists to dismiss him as a jazz player based on sound alone, yet despite the strong dance rhythm of the backing accompaniment, and the jazz flourishes of the clarinet solos, there's a lyrical, melancholy strain in "Interlude in B-Flat" that wouldn't be out of place in the music of the Impressionists – or Cole Porter. There are touches of Ravel and Debussy in the harmony, alongside Ford Dabney and Jelly Roll Morton; the melody recalls Weber's clarinet concertos. It's completely different to what Benny Goodman and other pioneers of big band and swing are playing at the time. In Shaw's opinion, the big dance bands are playing music that is at least a decade behind in jazz terms, and needs updating. It's this innovative quality that grabs the ears of the listeners when Artie premiers "Interlude in B-Flat" on 24 May 1936. When the four-minute piece is over, he gets a standing ovation. Yet that first success doesn't last. Artie records "Interlude in B-Flat" once, in 1936; that recording then disappears for the next 50 years. He still needs something to truly follow up on his breakthrough and push him into the limelight.

Artie's next stab at a signature composition is "Nightmare," composed the day before his band's scheduled opening at the Hotel Lexington on 21 August 1936, with a broadcast link to CBS radio. He's been told he needs a theme tune for the start and the end of the live broadcasts. "Nightmare" is a sinister A-minor escalation, sporting some elements that might have grown out of the Hasidic cantorial tradition, all relentless progression on trombones, sax and drum, and sudden menacing fanfares, with Artie interjecting on clarinet like a noir hero caught between inexorable forces. It lives up to its name. It's completely different in flavour from any other big band tune of the period, and totally distinctive.

The Hotel Lexington teaches Artie its own lesson about musical performance, though; not unlike the lesson that Cole Porter took away from the public reception of *Jubilee*. Artie's agent brings Charlie Rochester, the manager of the hotel, with aggrieved complaints that the band isn't doing a good job. Rochester points out that there are only about three people having dinner in the hall; no one dancing. Artie's job, he insists, is not to play good music, but to pull in customers. He tells Artie that he'll hire him to take off his pants and shit on the bandstand, so long as people come in and pay to see it. Artie listens, but doesn't necessarily learn. He takes his string band on the road, and encounters box-office washout after washout. By the end of 1937 his band's recording contract with Brunswick has lapsed, without renewal.

By March 1938, Artie has concluded that the only way for him to go is to beat the established players at their own game, and he pulls together a more conventional ensemble. He hires Billie Holiday, just a month after her split with the Count Basie Orchestra. Artie emphasizes that he's not doing it to make a political statement: Bille just happens to be the best singer available. All the same, the politics don't stay away. Artie insists on her touring with the band and appearing onstage like any other band member, even though this makes her one of the first black singers to work full time with a white orchestra. Billie doesn't always respect the arrogance of "Jesus Christ, King of the Clarinet, and His Band," but she does respect his musicianship. Together, they broadcast on New York's influential WABC station, and are so popular that they are given a return engagement in April. At Dartmouth's Green Key Prom in May 1938, Artie's band, with Billie Holiday singing, blows Tommy Dorsey's orchestra, America's favourite dance band, off the bandstand. Their tour schedule is hectic, from Philadelphia to Tennessee, bringing Artie and Billie into bruising contact with hecklers and segregated venues in the South.

Still searching for that breakthrough hit, Artie signs a new recording contract with RCA Victor. For one of the six tunes he's to record with his new 14-piece ensemble for RCA, he chooses an arrangement of "Begin the Beguine" that he's worked out with his arranger and orchestrator, Jerry Gray.

The song has had a chequered career since its premiere. When *Jubilee* sank, the song essentially went down with it. Josephine Baker danced to it in the *Ziegfield Follies of 1936,* on her return from Paris to America, but neither her performance nor the show were a great success. While Artie is on tour, a few diehard fans ask him if he knows how to play "Begin the Beguine." Artie is already a Cole Porter aficionado, who will record 19 Porter melodies throughout his career, more than any other artist. He is intrigued by the song's strangeness, and its sheer length: 104 bars and one constant melody, when most commercial songs are just 32 bars. Gray initially sticks to the original beguine rhythm, but Artie upgrades this to more of a four-four beat. Later, he pins down the secret of its success: "Begin the Beguine" is the first time that a jazz band, a swing ensemble, plays a melody instead of just a string of dance riffs. It has a melody, and you can dance to it. There's all the sophistication of Cole Porter's original lyrics, all the subtle poignancy of the major/minor shift, and the underlying dance floor punch, topped off by Artie's brilliant phrasing. From the arrangement's first airing at Boston's Roseland State Ballroom, the band know they have a hit. In an article published a year later, Artie writes: "Swing – and I mean *real* swing – is an idiom designed to make songs more listenable and danceable than they were in their original form." Obviously that's what he's done with "Begin the Beguine." It's the perfect distillation of awing.

RCA takes some convincing, though. They dismiss "Begin the Beguine" as a waste of time. After that first recording session on 24 July 1938, in the RCA Studio 2 on East 24th Street, they insist on releasing it as a smoothly contrasting B-side to Artie's scat-tinged version of "Indian Love Call" on the Bluebird Records label. The same session also produces Billie's only recorded track with Artie, and with RCA, the number "Any Old Time." Artie has a gift as a songwriter and lyricist that Cole Porter himself might have acknowledged, and "Any Old Time" is one of his most successful pieces. Billie's rendition is superb, but has to be withdrawn because her contract to Brunswick Records is still current.

In any case, it's "Begin the Beguine" that the public picks up on, and, in Artie's words, the B-side release takes off like a singed cat. Sales soar towards the millions. Autograph hunters hound Artie on the streets, and at every concert venue. In *Down Beat*'s poll for 1938, Artie dethrones Benny Goodman as reigning King of Swing. When Cole Porter meets Artie after the initial success of "Begin the Beguine," he shakes his hand and says, "Happy to meet my collaborator." Artie asks, "Did that involve royalties?" "No," Cole replies.

In October 1938 Artie is booked for a long-term engagement at the Blue Room in New York's Hotel Lincoln. Billie quits the band the following month, after the hotel asks her to use the service elevator instead of the passenger elevator, following complaints from white guests. Already she has been forbidden to go to the dining room or the bar with the rest of the band, and has had to enter and leave through the kitchen. She and Artie never work together again.

By January 1939, *Life* is running photo spreads of Artie's Hotel Lincoln residency. His band is enlarged and enriched by players of the calibre of George Auld and Buddy Rich. Artie is now also musical MC for the influential "Melody and Madness" program on CBS/WABC, introduced by Robert

Benchley, backed up by a slew of highly praised RCA Bluebird record releases. Fans mob him wherever he goes, to the point where he needs police protection. The onetime high school dropout is now earning $6,500 per week from theatre appearances – 100 times his income at the beginning of the year. His record contracts alone secure him an income of $100,000 for the next two years. WNEW's February poll rates him above Goodman, Tommy Dorsey, Count Basie, Gene Krupa and Duke Ellington as most popular swing band. Paramount, Warner Brothers and other movie studios are vying for him. His newfound fame is taking its toll, however. He's on a treadmill of touring, performing, broadcasting, songwriting, arranging, editing and film appearances. Something has to give.

In March 1939 Artie follows Robert Benchley's show to Los Angeles and is booked for the Palomar Ballroom in Hollywood. On the first night at the Palomar on 19 April, opening to a record crowd, he collapses with a sore throat and is rushed to hospital. He's already had an advance warning in September 1938 with a similar collapse at WNEW during a "Battle of the Bands" program alongside the bands of Tommy Dorsey, Claude Hopkins and Merle Pit. Feverish and unconscious for days, he is diagnosed with malignant leukopenia and given only a slim chance of recovery. When he awakens five days later, Artie finds his Hollywood friend Judy Garland at his bedside. He is a star.

Chapter 9

John is pleasantly surprised that Farah gets his first letter at all. When he reads her reply, he is no longer surprised, but alarmed. It's not so much over concern that she's taken his offer of help seriously. It's that he can't help realizing how intelligent she is – and how inferior that makes him feel.

The close camaraderie of the sea, and the even more constrained society of a Cunard liner, have not helped John develop much perspective on such things. For him, like any other sailor, a master's certificate outweighs any university degree, and a professional mariner who performs all his duties competently has as much learning as anyone could ever reasonably expect. And yet suddenly here is this young girl, not yet out of her teens, asking him what pure mathematical electives he would recommend to go with her main course, as though knowledge of celestial navigation and tide tables had equipped him to be her tutor. It's embarrassing.

John sends a temporizing reply by the next mailboat, and resorts to the ship's library. What began as a casual, half-flirtatious offer starts to assume far more serious proportions. John now has something to keep him occupied during those long off-watches at sea, and reason to exercise his mind beyond the narrow demands of seamanship. He sends letters to his father, asking him to make inquiries at the University on Farah's behalf. He starts to pursue study for the sheer pleasure of it, patronizing the ship's circulating library, whiling away passages between Cape Town and Rio over his books.

It's just as well John has so much free time on his hands, because Farah takes some keeping up with. Her letters are as frank and sweet as he'd expect from a girl of her age and background, but when she does bring up mathematics, it's usually the theory of statistics, and especially how much she's learned by delving back into the ancient work of Arab mathematicians, the original founders of the science.

Dear Mr Graham,

It's most thoughtful of you to give up your valuable time to help me with my maths. I'm sure you must have much more important things to do. But I do appreciate it very much, and I hope I can achieve something in good time that will make you feel that your time was not wasted, God willing.

Did you know, by the way, that the Persian mathematician Sharaf al-Dīn al-Tūsī wrote some of the earliest versions of differential calculus, in his Treatise on Equations? Six centuries before Newton and Leibniz. Of course, I would never question the merits of the great masters of the science, but all the same, it is fascinating, don't you think?

I hope you are keeping well and safe at sea. Life here is as dull as ever apart from schoolwork; no more dances. The teachers keep us at our books. And a propos, I must stop now and study. May this find you well,

Yours truly,
Farah Ayad

John can't yet follow her into the mathematical intricacies of the work of Al-Khalil and Al-Kindi, but he starts to develop a fascination for the intellectual history of that period, and its scientific and cultural achievements, especially as so much of it encroaches onto astronomy and celestial navigation.

Ever since he started naming the stars in the heavens, John has wondered at how many of them have Arab names, and as he learned to steer by them, that wonderment has only increased. Now he begins to follow the genesis of his own science, the fruits of the House of Wisdom and the dismantling of the Ptolemaic system; the early celestial globes and armillary spheres; the great star catalogues of Baghdad and Samarkand. Azimuth, zenith and nadir reassume their ancient Arabic origins. He's found a point of common interest with Farah that he can discuss with her without feeling too overshadowed by her precocious brilliance. Their letters start to resemble a curious sequence of celestial diagrams, like pages from some medieval grimoire.

John receives a duplicate copy of the admissions papers for the University of Glasgow, and starts an extended long-distance consultation with Farah once she's received her copy, going over the requirements. The long lists of qualifications look as forbidding to him as ever, but Farah assures him that she can match them. The other major requirement, convincing her family, is her affair, and one where he can't help. Fortunately, it turns out that her parents are impressed by the well-established, and well-regulated and supervised, residential arrangements for lady students at the University; for that reason alone, Glasgow is already turning out to be a fortuitous choice. Farah manages to discreetly slide into the family discussions at just the right time the fact that one of the visiting Cunard officers is aware of her ambitions and has been helping her out. Cunard is enough of a guarantee of cachet, discretion and respectability to mollify her parents about the news that she has been in correspondence with a man.

The flow of letters continues almost interrupted, although the days and sometimes weeks that pass between mail deliveries at least give John time to catch up on his studies. He helps Farah draft her application letters, double-checks her choices of subjects, reads the recommended background literature himself to be sure to give the best advice. He's almost living the scholastic life vicariously through her. She takes up practically all his time outside his studies and his duties. The thought of dallying with any other woman never even enters his head.

Finally, one delirious staccato telegram arrives, informing him she's been accepted by the University of Glasgow on a Seychelles scholarship, to study Political Economy. John's heart swells with vicarious pride. Farah has less time to write to him in the ensuing few months, during the whirlwind of preparation prior to her departure for Glasgow. He does manage to see her for one evening during the *Franconia*'s latest winter cruise. There's one terribly strict, terribly proper, terribly correct formal tea with the family, with John terribly stiff in full dress uniform, terribly self-conscious and sweating even more than usual in the tropical heat, as Farah's parents make small talk over Earl Grey with lemon and ask him delicately probing questions about his work, his background, his parents, his religion, and so on. Luckily, they warm to the news that his mother is Roman Catholic: Farah's mother is apparently impressed with the tight discipline and propriety at the Catholic girls' schools, and sees this as some kind of confirmation of good behaviour. A certain aspirational snobbery in Farah's father does John no harm either: a marine officer, practically a Naval officer if one's being broad-minded, is a figure to reckon with in an island community like the Seychelles, especially one who guides the great white liners that are the island's most conspicuous brush with the wider world's pinnacles of sophistication and civilization. As a medical man, Farah's father also shares the technical mindset: John has no difficulty convincing him of the value of his work, where a deck steward or even a staff captain might have stumbled. Farah herself is ebullient, and carries the whole evening with her sheer enthusiasm. John leaves with a distinct feeling of being on probation, but with good marks so far.

When Farah does leave her birthplace to take up her place at the University, it's not in the luxurious comfort of the *Franconia*, but on a regular steamship. Still, John is able to secure her a better quality cabin, and makes sure of her safety and comfort at every stop along the way. In Glasgow itself, her parents make acceptance by one of the women's halls of residence a precondition of her taking up the course; fortunately, Queen Margaret Hall, the oldest and best established, has a place for her. Farah is not the novelty she would be further south, with the University graduating its first female Asian student, Dr Marbai Ardesir Vakil, in 1897. By the 1930s she's practically a commonplace among the other students in the Department of Political Economy, itself the purview of a succession of distinguished women teachers, starting with Theodora Keith in 1919 and N.M. Scott in 1921. Her first letters after she arrives are as breathless and avid as any young girl at Christmas time. John can't shake off the association in his mind of Glasgow with dull chill, but now it's as though he was looking at it once again through the enchanted eyes of childhood.

Farah seems completely comfortable with her housemates and her surroundings, and fascinated by her studies. All the same, once she's thoroughly settled in and the initial novelty of student life has worn off, John becomes conscious of a poignant, yearning tone on both sides that he hadn't been aware of before. They've grown so close during the eager months of preparation and anticipation, and now that she's reached her goal, it seems to have pushed them apart again. In purely practical terms, he's kept at sea for the duration of the cruises in the winter and the ransatlantic crossings in the summer, and can't take time to see her, which they both realize, even if they don't fully express it, is something they both badly want.

At last, John gets a convenient spell of home leave in the autumn, and arranges to see Farah while he's staying with his parents. She has already met the family, briefly, for tea in Sauciehall Street, and won their approval. John schedules to take her out from her lodgings for tea and a walk in Kelvingrove Park below the University. On leave and out of uniform, he's determined to prove to Farah that he can carry himself off as well in civilian dress, not that she ever brought up the topic. Scottish weather being as it is, though, he has to put on his bridge coat, rather incongruous with a scarf and a plain cap. Mother insists on him wearing the scarf and cap, and on making sure that he's wrapped up well against the cold.

It's a typical Glasgow autumn day, overcast pearl grey with glints of silver-gilt where the sun peeks through, when he catches the train to Finnieston to walk up to Kelvingrove Park, dodging the trams in Argyle Street, and thence to the University. The trees in the park are arrayed in the panoply of autumn: copper and bronze, with scarlet and orange lappets, leaves littering the paths like shed greaves after a rout. The University's great latticework spire, looming over the park, seems to shake an admonitory finger at him as he comes; part chiding him for seeking to rob its sanctum of its virgin treasure;

part reproving him for daring to tread in its sacred precincts without an appropriate qualification. Regardless, he presses on and up the hill, past students in tweeds and Oxford bags, and asks the porter on duty outside the main gate on University Avenue for directions to Queen Margaret Hall. Round the back of the Hunterian Art Gallery he finds the low reddish building with its ornate classical portico, and asks another glowering porter to fetch Farah out.

When Farah emerges, she's wearing a bonnet, an actual tam cap, in a dark tartan that John doesn't recognize. It looks extraordinarily becoming on her thick, dark hair.

"Are ye sure ye'll be warm enough like that," John asks, suddenly uncertain whether he should be taking her out at all in this cold weather.

"Oh, I'll be fine," she replies, ducking her head in a little bob like a questing moorhen, as she takes his proffered arm. "I'm not the fragile tropic bloom you take me for, John Graham."

"Are you not?" he answers, tickled. "So I suppose you're quite at home here already now, are you?"

"Oh, it has its charms compared to home," she confirms, and, pursing her lips, blows a white plume of breath out into the cold Glasgow air, smiling in delight at the result. "You'd never see that back there."

"You wouldn't," he chuckles. "Not that I miss it when I'm out there. Seems a strange turnabout, you up here in the chill and the Glasgow smirr, and me down there sailing the tropic seas."

"Well, don't go thinking you're any less of a Scot, no matter where you sail, John Graham: you still look every inch the tall white boy to me," she chides him, a twinkle in her eye. There's a slight Caledonian lilt to her speech now, something she's evidently picked up while she's been here. John finds it charming, though even more disorienting.

"I thought we could take a walk through the park, and perhaps have some tea," he declares. "I'll make sure to have you back at your lodgings at the right hour."

"Still keeping your watches, even on shore." She pouts slightly. "You know I love it here, but I still look forward to your letters? You could write more often, you know. I'm sure that deck duty doesn't take up so much of your time."

"Oh, I'm sorry, I didn't realize. I'll try, I promise."

"Mind you do, now." She prods his arm, and then takes it. They walk arm in arm across Professor's Square. The sky has cleared a little more now, and yellow shafts of sunshine are lighting up the pinnacles of the University Chapel and Wards Library. Farah feels as light as an autumn leaf on his arm, but the warm weight and pressure of her impresses itself on him at every step. She trembles slightly, and he stops for a moment, concerned.

"Are you sure you feel alright coming out? I don't want you catching a chill. Allah knows what your parents would say."

Farah shrugs. "I'm fine, really. I'm quite comfortable here. I wrap up well and I watch my diet. I even drink that tea they serve in Lady Margaret Hall. It may be slop, but it keeps you warm in the colder months."

"You do seem very at home here, I must say."

"I am." She smiles, looking away from him for a moment, wistfully. "You know it does make a good change from Port Victoria. Now don't give me that look: I know it seems like paradise, and in many ways it is, but compared to Glasgow, it's unending monotony. It lulls you to sleep. And it's an island, and no matter how wide its horizons seems, its coasts are narrow. It's a very, very little world. A young girl could be forgiven for wanting to get out and see a bit more of things, don't you think?"

"I daresay. Glasgow might be thought a queer choice, though. Not exactly a fairytale romance, is it?"

"It'll do for me." She smiles at him again, and again there's that look in her eye that he can't quite place, the twinkle that dares you to look deeper to see where the light is coming from. "You know you haven't had it so bad yourself, if only you'd realize. I liked Clydebank when I went to call on your parents. Oh, I know it's grim and industrial, but it's neighbourly too. And if you just look across the Clyde to the far bank, or up towards the hills, it's lovely. You should see some of the shanties back home compared to the streets there, with their fine brick and stone houses. Maybe next time you call, go take a look."

At the foot of the hill, they cross the footbridge over the rushing current of the River Kelvin, and stroll along Argyle Street to the Kelvingrove Art Gallery. The sky is clearing now, and the monumental Gallery's red Locharbriggs sandstone glows warmly in the sunshine. John leads Farah up the steps, and to the cafe in the Centre Hall. He orders tea. The concert pipe organ above the far end of the hall is playing a medley of popular tunes, including "Tea for Two" and "Night and Day." At the latter, he glances at Farah, and notices that she's been looking at him all this time. She flushes and lowers her eyes.

"You remember…" he begins.

"Of course I remember," she cuts him off. "Not likely to forget now, am I? I should be sad if you were to think of me as that flighty, John Graham."

"With you at the University, studying the way you are?" he chuckles incredulously. "That's the last thing I'd think."

She shrugs. "It's nothing. Just hard work, that's all."

"Well, I think it's admirable nonetheless. In fact, I was giving some thought as to whether I should quit the Service, or at least ask for an extended leave, and enrol at a university myself."

That gets her attention. "Would you?" she asks, fixing him with her deep brown stare. "I mean, would you give up the high life and all that luxury for dusty books and bad tea?"

"Oh, it's not at all as luxurious as it looks. Most of that is just show, for the passenger decks. Down below, it's mostly a mix of boredom with the occasional bit of danger. Honestly, the one part I really enjoy is the sailing and navigation."

"Danger?" she picks up on that, and leaves the word hanging in the air."

"Oh, not often, but there is some. Accidents, broken bones, men lost overboard, or suicides, fatal illnesses. We had a couple die of malaria last trip. The captain is still scratching his head and sending off letters about where they might have caught it."

"And you didn't think to tell me?" Her voice is unexpectedly sharp, and John looks round to see that her face is flushed and her jaw set in anger. "How can you be so careless? All that time at sea, and never a word about it? Think what could have happened to you. At least make sure you take your quinine pills, or tonic water, or Dubonnet, or whatever it is they prescribe for you these days."

Surprised by her fervour, John does his best to look contrite. "I promise, I'll take all the precautions I can. I was already, honestly. I'm not foolish enough to ignore malaria outbreaks in the tropics."

"You'd better," she admonishes him. He wishes he could laugh it off, but she looks completely serious, something very fixed and determined in her expression. Women are such a mystery, he concludes.

After that outburst, conversation takes a little while to pick up again, with awkward pauses and hesitant pleasantries. But he can't keep mum around Farah for very long. When the tea and cakes are finished, they tour the galleries, mostly just to pass the time, as neither of them is especially artistic. They stop for a moment before Rubens and Brueghel's "Nature and Her Followers," to admire the lush fecundity of the fruit and flower garlands framing the picture. Farah remarks that they remind her of home. John is more focused on the voluptuous pink forms of the nymphs and Graces. He notices that Farah's dark cheeks are slightly flushed, and he wonders.

Once outside the Gallery, they stroll along the lanes of the park, arm in arm. The sky has cleared completely, and bright sunshine sets the autumn foliage ablaze, the towers and spires of the Gallery and the University aglow. "It's like a fairy tale," Farah breathes.

"So is this your dream of romance?" he asks, smiling down at her. Somehow he doesn't dread the comparison, now that he's here with her on his arm, however much he always feels in awe of her when he's far away at sea answering her letters.

"It's good enough for me," she smiles winsomely. Even though her skin is hardly that dark, and has lightened conspicuously during her sojourn up north, just a shade below cafe au lait, her teeth still gleam brightly against her complexion. He bends down and kisses her gently on the lips. Just as hesitantly, she responds. The moment passes without either of them fully registering what's just happened. Unthinkingly, they draw that much closer together on the walk back up the hill to Queen Margaret Hall, and he kisses her goodbye spontaneously as though it's the most natural thing in the world.

John still has a couple more days of his leave, and he proposes to take Farah out dancing. She accepts. That puts him into a fluster he hadn't anticipated when he popped the question. For one thing, he doesn't have any evening dress. His mother sorts that out, pulling his father's old dress suit out of the back of the wardrobe, although it needs considerable airing to get rid of the smell of mothballs. He's also suddenly, terribly concerned about his dance steps. The occasional dance on shipboard or at one of the stops en route hasn't very well prepared him, although Farah certainly didn't complain at that first dance in Port Victoria. He decides to take her to the Imperial Palais on St George's Road: it's closer to the West End, Woodlands and Kelvinbridge than most of the other leading dance halls, and hence a little more up-market. Still, he would never dream of asking a young woman in full evening dress and high heels to walk even the short distance from the University, and so he calls for her in a taxi at seven, his hair freshly brilliantined, an orchid in his buttonhole. With Queen Margaret Hall's strict curfews, he has to have her back by nine, but all the same, with autumn's early twilight this far north, it already feels like a full night out.

Farah is wearing a dark, demure dress under her coat, with covered shoulders, and plain shoes, rather sober and understated. To his eyes, she looks lovely; suddenly he's conscious that he no longer has a precocious girl by his side, but a woman. The straight-backed taxi whisks them eastwards in relative silence, but she holds his hand the whole way. Even on a Saturday night, the line at the entrance to the dance hall is relatively short at this time of the evening, and he already has tickets in his breast pocket. The band whose music greets them as they check their coats is not the first-rank orchestra of one of the bigger halls in prime season; not Joe Loss or Lauri Blandford, but is still serviceable enough: the Glasgow dance hall circuit is crowded and fiercely competitive, and a substandard outfit would never survive. Before leading her to a table overlooking the sparsely populated dance floor, he orders drinks at the bar: a gin and tonic for himself, a plain lime soda for her. The band is playing "Tomorrow's Another Day."

"All right till nine?" he confirms, checking his watch.

"Ever the dutiful sailor," she giggles. "Don't worry: I've got my permission from the warden. We can relax and enjoy the evening."

"I'm not so worried about the warden," he demurs. "If I ever got you into trouble with your parents, I don't think I'd be able to forgive myself."

"Oh, hush now." She sips her lime soda, watching the few daring couples already circling below them. "I want to enjoy the experience while I've got it. This is better than dancing to the gramophone in the club, with Mummy and Daddy playing Vingt-et-Un with the other members and keeping an eye on me."

Obviously ready to kick off the real business of the evening, the bandleader announces Count Basie's "Jumpin' at the Woodside." That's enough to get quite a few more couples onto the floor. They stay on even when the band slows the tempo with Larry Clinton's "My Reverie," which feels to John like the right moment to take Farah's arm and lead her out. Thanks to her natural grace, he manages not to make too much of a hash of leading off. They stay on the floor for "Music, Maestro, Please" by Tommy Dorsey, then the bandleader makes a short, almost reverential pause before announcing "Begin the Beguine." By now the dancefloor is quite full, and John holds Farah close to him, so when their eyes meet in recognition at the first few bars, she's looking up at him from where her head is resting against his chest.

"I'd say 'They're playing our song,' but it seems like it's

everywhere and everybody's now," she murmurs to him. "I never thought I'd be dancing to it like this, though, with you."

John holds her to him, and swings her through the rest of the number, and Gershwin's "Nice Work If You Can Get It," and the tune after that. They'd never make great dancers, he knows, but they make a good couple, and that's all that matters to him. He's never felt more comfortable with a girl, more in the right place. Farah fits perfectly in his arms like she belongs there, and the warmth of her breasts filling the space between them is a delight. To rest his jaw against her hair, with her chin on his collar bone, is a joy past compare. It also keeps the clock face above the dance floor in sight, though, and he sees the minutes ticking by. No matter how delicious it is to feel her against him, he wants to talk with her as well, and he's losing that opportunity as the hour draws near when he'll have to give her up. Finally, as "Thanks for the Memory" reaches its last few bars, he leads her off the floor and to the cloakroom.

"Let's take a walk and I'll find you a taxi," he tells her. Farah nods regretfully, and takes her coat from the attendant. Outside, the night is clear but not too chilly for the time of year, and the stars are out between the streetlights. John leads her across North Street to Woodside Crescent, where they can enjoy the walk under the trees along the Georgian facades of Woodside Terrace and Park Gardens. If they had come out later, the night would have been colder and the walk an ordeal, but for once the short time they have together has worked in their favour. Farah huddles against his bridge coat, and he takes off his father's slightly yellowed white silk scarf and wraps it around her shoulders. They pause on Park Terrace where the view across the park opens up to disclose the glimmer of the University towers across the River Kelvin, and the more distant, brighter lights of Plantation, Govan and Ibrox across the Clyde, and above their heads, the stars.

"It doesn't bother you, does it?" Farah asks, shivering slightly as she hugs him, but uncomplaining and in no hurry to let go.

"What doesn't?" he asks, bemused.

"That I'm Muslim," she says in a small voice, lowering her

head.

"Why should it? Here, look up at the stars." He turns her in his arms so her back is pressed against him, and tilts her head up to look at the sky. "Achenar," he pronounces, kissing her on the back of her neck with each name. "Mizar. Spica. Deneb. Aldebaran."

She sighs and droops in his arms, leaning back. "It's not as simple as that, darling. Mummy always chided me that I wasn't pious enough, that I'd come to a bad end."

"Hush, we'll cross that bridge when we come to it." He turns her back to face him, and kisses her full on the lips.

With just a short time in hand, he hails a cab cruising along the Terrace, and huddles with her in the back of the taxi for the short drive back to Queen Margaret Hall, leaving her on the doorstep with a final kiss and moments to spare. All the way back to the station, all the way on the train back to Clydebank, he holds his scarf and his coat close around him, to smell her lingering perfume on the fabric.

After that leave, their correspondence is no longer so formal and correct, no longer so scholarly. John is as little at home in the language of romance as any technically-minded Scot, but he does his heartfelt best. And every new letter from Farah brings a leap to his heart; every mail delivery that goes by without one is a keen disappointment. Not that there are that many disappointments now: she writes often, volubly, passionately, keeping him up to date on her studies and her days, but chiefly letting her heart pour out her feelings. John had never expected first love to be like this; had never thought about it much at all before: now he's swept away by it.

Dearest:-

It seems like ages since I wrote to you, but I know it was just last week when I was out on the banks of Loch Lomond. I'm back in the city now, and hard at work as ever, and looking forward to your next letter to lighten the gloom. You know the Glasgow weather is so changeable at this time of year, especially for a tropic bird like me, but there was a letter waiting there from you, and that made even a back inside room look bright and cheerful to me. I am glad to hear that the latest stop at Mombasa went well, and that you were "well turned out," according to your captain's standards. You always are in my eyes, and I hope, in his. You must, must take care of yourself and keep to the smarter parts of town; don't go getting yourself into any trouble or catching malaria. You need to trust my knowledge on this; these towns are all the same.

I went into Glasgow Cathedral yesterday; Daddy would not have approved, I know, but I have kept up my prayers, so I felt I was still a pious enough girl to survive contact with the infidel. How silly we all are, aren't we? It looked very plain and ordinary on the outside, but oh so grand on the inside – pure Gothic, like something straight out of Walter Scott. While I was in there, I said a prayer for you in my heart – I said it to Allah, but I felt I was in the right place. I don't know if it will help, but I do hope so. The news is so grim, as if shipwreck and typhoons weren't enough to worry about. The Union and the Debating Society have become very gloomy and angry places these days. I must stop now, but do take care of your dearest self and write to me again soon.

• *Your affectionate Farah*

John tries to brighten her gloom with all the letters he can write, but their face-to-face meetings during his leaves are all too brief and hesitant. The *Franconia* is spending more time cruising in northern waters – Norway, Sweden, Iceland, even Leningrad – but that seems to give him all too little leave time at home, and all too little time to see her. John is still at sea for her graduation, though he telegrams her with effusive congratulations when she graduates with flying colours, and loves the pictures she posts back for him: her looking very proper and distinguished in her gown and hood, holding her rolled diploma. He's still at sea when she leaves Scotland for the last time, with a tearful farewell to the University, to Queen Margaret Hall, and to his family, and sails home to the Seychelles.

John is too preoccupied with Farah to pay more than cursory attention to the appointment in June of a new captain for the *Franconia*: James Gordon Partridge Bisset, a veteran of RMS *Carpathia*'s rescue of the *Titanic* survivors. They exchange more letters than ever, and he plans to see her again on the forthcoming winter cruise, once he's once again round the Cape of Good Hope and east of Suez. Then one day comes the news that cuts across all their plans. It's the first of September 1939, and war has been declared.

Chapter 10

On 23 May 1939, recovered from his illness, Artie returns to the "Melody and Madness" series, broadcasting from the NBC Studios at Sunset & Vine, and to the Palomar Ballroom, where his band has been doing record business in his absence. In June, he plays at the International Jitterbug Championships at the Los Angeles Memorial Coliseum, before a crowd of 26,000. He still isn't entirely over his brush with death, though, and at the end of the month he has a tonsillectomy, fortunately making a full recovery.

That's just as well, because by this time, Artie and his band are contracted for two movies, Metro's *Broadway Melody of 1940*, with Fred Astaire and Eleanor Powell, and Robert Benchley continuing his relation with Artie as principal comedy lead, and MGM's *Dancing Co-Ed,* with the young Lana Turner. Filming on both takes place in July. Artie and his band continue to prop up the "Music and Madness" radio show, without Benchley, and tour through much of August, in Kansas City, Chicago, Grand Rapids, and other Midwest venues. At one stop on the tour, in St. Louis, he reveals to the *St. Louis Post-Dispatch* that he feels he's "gone as far as I can with band playing our present style. What I'd like to do is organize an American symphonic band to play American music in the swing idiom or jazz idiom or whatever you want to call it." On 19 August Artie is scheduled to play an outdoor concert on Boston Common, in front of a crowd of some 10,000. After the concert, the Mayor of Boston attempts to drive Artie away in his limousine, escorted by 40 police. The crowd stops the car, and overturns the limousine. Artie escapes the car and fights his way through the crowd back to his hotel, arriving with some of his clothes torn off. On 4 September, a near riot breaks out among 2,500 fans in Buffalo, Ontario, when Artie and his band walk out in a dispute over payments. His salary now reputedly runs at around $14,000, and his Hollywood film appearances have reportedly fetched him another $100,000.

MGM releases *Dancing Co-Ed* late September. Publicity stills for the film show Lana Turner leaning against Artie's back and high-kicking as he blows his horn. Almost concurrently, Artie gives an interview to Michael Mok of the *New York Post*, where he declares that: "I hate the music business, and I'll tell you why. In a month and a half they haven't given me a minute to work out something worthwhile with my band... And I don't like the crowds. I'm not interested in giving people what they want. I'm interested in making music. Autograph hunters? To hell with them!... If I was made by a bunch of morons, that's just too bad." As for Hollywood, "I like Hollywood but I detest the picture business and most of the people in it. It's one big continuous one-night stand in Podunk." In the same interview, Artie adds that he loves the work of Lafcadio Hearn, and "used to be interested in Communism... As I understand it, the ultimate objective of Communism, in its pure form, is to give people leisure to express themselves in arts and skills. I have come to the conclusion that too much leisure is no good. If Hitler had stuck to his house-painting job and was now swinging a brush ten hours a day, he wouldn't have time to dream of power."

Artie does sometimes have less condescending moments. *Variety* remarks on his stage demeanour at the time: "Shaw relies on his music and his labors. Without pushing the personality equation, his modest manner is on the whole very pleasant and he makes a neat appearance. His announcements are fairly good and his diction dear. No stunts, no comedy, no trick dressing or other devices, the formula followed is one of giving forth lots and hot."

All the same, those remarks catch up with him. In October, the longstanding "Music and Madness" show parts company with Artie and his band; the odd splicing of radio comedy with a top swing band has long since outworn its welcome. Some reports claim that Artie's remarks about his fans in the *New York Post* prompted the show to fire him. *Down Beat* brings up reports of Artie snubbing journalists and fans, of late appearances, and speculates that he may quit the music business entirely as soon as he's financially set for life. All the negative publicity doesn't seem to have done Artie and the band any harm when he opens their new engagement at Café Rouge in New York's Hotel Pennsylvania on 19 October, to a packed house, with Artie himself playing the genial host to guests and autograph-hunters. On 28 October, though, Artie vents in a long letter to *Billboard*, complaining about the few rowdy jitterbugs, with "no consideration for anyone but themselves," who spoil things for the majority. "Wherever you congregate a group of 500 or 1,000 young people you'll always find a few who try to hog the limelight. Either they're destructive and call attention to themselves by breaking chairs and overturning tables or defacing walls, or they'll try to give the impression a band has been hired to play for their particular benefit. They're the proverbial soreheads who want everything their way." Artie takes time to extol "the rest of the patrons who listen and dance to swing – all I can say is that THEY have made swing what it is."

In late October, Artie is also hit with a lawsuit, an action for $30,000 damages initiated by Eli E. Oberstein, a former manager of artists at RCA-Victor, who alleges that Artie owes him a share of earnings for 1937 and 1938. Artie responds that the agreement entitling Oberstein to a share of his earnings was extracted under duress, and that he was threatened with the loss of his RCA-Victor contract if he did not sign. Whatever the merits of the case, it obviously adds to the stress that Artie is under, and contributes to what happens next.

On 18 November 1939 Artie summons his band to his room at the Hotel Pennsylvania, and tells them "I've had it." Later he explains that he's fed up with the uphill battle of fighting audience expectations in order to get some music played. He tells the *Saturday Evening Post*: "I learned during my illness on the Coast that while a quarter of a million will buy a lot of things, it won't buy the energy you blew making it. Irregular hours, no recreation, food on the run, and nervous tension will get you sooner or later."

Artie's band forms a cooperative to continue for the present, with saxophonist George Auld leading. Artie himself heads off in a red Packard, taking his manager along some of the way, and eventually winds up south of the Rio Grande in Acapulco. On 2 December, an article written by him with Bob Maxwell appears in the *Saturday Evening Post*. There, Artie vents about the state of the music business and the power of managers, booking offices and music publishers. "The leader who accepts help of this kind is always in debt to those who helped him. He'll have to give his publisher-benefactor's songs a plug whether they're good or bad. He'll have to record tunes he knows aren't worth putting on wax. He's owned, musically, and he does his owner's bidding." Artie has long ago deduced that "it was financial suicide to try to sell the public on anything novel without tremendous backing." Instead he has to "beat the topnotchers at their own game." He concludes: "I never should have been a success or made money in the music business. Having broken every rule and regulation for subservience, having fed the public songs everyone was convinced the public didn't want to hear, I should have been out in the cold a long time ago. Some big people in the business think I'm either cracked or a poseur. They refuse to believe that, with me, music is first."

Chapter 11

The autumn and winter of 1939, and the spring of 1940, may be the Phoney War for Britain and France as a whole, but not for the *Franconia*. She is immediately requisitioned by H.M. Government for service as a troopship after her arrival in Liverpool from New York on 12 September 1939, and begins a refit. By 25 September, newly painted grey, with most of her splendid interior fittings stripped out and put into storage, she's off on her first wartime voyage, bound for Southampton. There she takes on troops, then sets sail for East Africa, to reinforce British forces against the threat of attack from Mussolini's armies in Africa Orientale Italiana. Her passengers include Ralph Bagnold, African explorer and future founder of the Long Range Desert Group.

John naturally sails with her. Wartime requires no wholesale remanning of the ship, no replacement of the deck department and the engineering department. Even some of the stewards stay on to man the catering department essential for her new role as a troopship. They're all given the choice to stay on with the *Franconia* or serve ashore, or in another branch of the Armed Forces; more than enough decide to stay with the ship. Wartime and her exterior coat of grey paint notwithstanding, the *Franconia* still retains something of her pre-war luxury polish and *esprit de corps*. With so many of the catering department opting to stay on the ship, she can still provide a level of service and comfort for her passengers quite beyond the usual troopship – at least for the upper ranks. Officers eat off white linen with real silverware, while even the other ranks below decks, although they endure considerably worse food and less comfort, eat actual white bread, rather than the greyish substitute becoming increasingly familiar elsewhere. It's all been provided for. The well-planned, well-subsidized role of the great shipping lines as the sinews of Empire is coming into its own once again.

John has his duty as her third officer, and is fated to stay with his ship and go where she goes. He manages to get off a quick letter to Farah, with no idea how long it will take to actually reach her, and no chance of including details on his journey or destination. Censorship is an all-too-recent memory from the last war, and John knows his duty. On every leg of his voyages, Farah will be left worrying with no more than a hint of where he is or what awaits him.

My dearest Farah,
Written in great haste, love: We are setting sail. Everything is too confused for me to be able to tell you anything. Things should settle down later. Take care of yourself, sweetheart. God knows how long this mess will last, but perhaps it will be less than we think. With all my love, darling, John

John spares her even more worry, but he has the whole Cunard heritage from World War 1 to remind him of the toll that wartime takes on the merchant marine. Casualty rates in the Merchant Navy will surpass one in four – higher than almost any other arm of the services – through the entire duration of the war, and the first months are the worst. John has that chance of dying every time he boards ship.

Fortunately perhaps, John is off watch when, after she enters the Mediterranean, the *Franconia* collides on 5 October with one of her sister ships, the RMS *Alcantara*, a former Royal Mail Lines liner, converted at Admiralty behest into an armed merchant cruiser. The *Alcantara,* apparently mistaking port for starboard, runs straight into the *Franconia*. Both ships are damaged in the collision, and the *Franconia* limps into Malta for repairs, offloading her cargo of troops. By December she's back in Liverpool, allowing John to spend some welcome days of leave with his family, and to catch up with correspondence from Farah. His letter-writing opportunities are strictly rationed at sea, and now is a chance to spend a little more time on writing. Farah has been sending her letters to his parents, rather than try to catch up with the *Franconia*, and he has weeks' worth of letters waiting for him. At least the war doesn't seem to be affecting the Seychelles much: Farah mostly just complains of boredom and stultifying home life. After Glasgow and the opening of the gates of opportunity for her, she's galled to have them slammed shut again. She's trying to get war work at Government House with her new qualifications, assisting local administration. Her parents have taken to dropping hints about marriage, and she's doing her best to put them off. They also ask after John, but it's obvious that they no longer are sure of what he is to her. Nothing is certain in wartime.

1940 begins for John with weeks of frustration, inaction and boredom at Birkenhead, barring one short voyage to the Clyde in March for another blissful few days at home. By April, though, he's at sea again with far more purpose. The *Franconia* sets sail on 3 April from Birkenhead to the Clyde. As First Sea Lord, Winston Churchill is already marshalling forces for Plan R 4, an expedition in force to neutral Norway, but Germany beats him to the punch and turns the Phoney War all too genuine by launching its invasion of Norway on the day of the *Franconia*'s departure.

From the Clyde, the *Franconia* sails for Norway, carrying troops and a labour force to relieve the British forces in the Narvik campaign. For John, it brings back memories of transatlantic crossings when spindrift blasted his face like gravel and the stewards rushed to bolt down the wardroom furniture. On the voyage out, he catches sight of a Lapp reindeer herdsman, apparently oblivious to all the chaos and confusion of wartime, swimming with his reindeer just off the Norwegian shore.

The *Franconia* arrives at the port of Harstad just north of Narvik on 20 April, escorted by the battle-cruiser *Repulse,* and the destroyers *Havant, Havelock* and *Fame*, but the congestion in the port is so severe that over 1,140 men of the labour force she's carrying have to return with her to Britain without ever disembarking. At least she's able to take on wounded and POWs for the return voyage. On the homeward leg of her voyage, early in the morning of 26 April, sailing unescorted, *Franconia* is attacked by a German U-boat. The destroyers

Janus and *Antelope* are dispatched from Scapa Flow to assist her, but when they find her safe and undamaged, they return to port, and the *Franconia* arrives back in the Clyde the next day.

John remembers the blissful days when the *Franconia* was unchallenged queen of the waves, alone in a sapphire ocean, neither land nor other vessel in sight, cruising in complete liberty. Now she's never alone. In her holds and cabins, soldiers are quartered everywhere there's space: hung in hammocks like so many dead fish, more men sleeping on pallets and tables beneath the hammocks, crammed into deathtraps of holds accessible only via narrow companion-ladders. The open seas around her offer no relief. Whether it's the distant, unwelcome attentions of enemy U-boats or aircraft, or the close attentions of escorts and convoy masters, she's always being scrutinized and harried.

The *Franconia*, alas, is one of the slower vessels in the merchant fleet, keeping an average 16 knots in convoy while many of her sister ships manage more than 20, and that puts even more of an onus on her to keep up and not fall out of formation or delay the passage. All signals are by lamps or flags to maintain radio silence; all ships have to stay on station at night in complete blackout, without riding lights. Every watch becomes a grinding struggle to keep station, avoid collision, maintain a lookout, heed signals, stay on course, take evasive action, zigzag, obey the Senior Officer Present, in the teeth of whatever conditions the ocean can throw at them. An average separation of two thirds of a mile between ships can diminish to almost nothing with frightening speed in darkness or bad weather. Poor visibility, poorer seamanship, confused and contradictory orders, are far more persistent foes than the Axis; constant strain and tedium far more prevalent than fear. John takes to sleeping in his clothes, and often wears three to four days' worth of stubble. The old Cunard punctilio has gone sadly by the board, but no one complains about that. Readiness matters far more.

On 10 May 1940, Germany invades the Netherlands and Belgium. Britain's performance in Norway has already brought down Neville Chamberlain's government in the Norway Debate, and Churchill becomes Prime Minister the same day. On 14 May, the *Franconia* sets sail again, this time in convoy with her sister ship the *Lancastria*, carrying a Canadian infantry brigade to relieve the Royal Marines who have just occupied Iceland in a *fait accompli* engineered by Winston Churchill, regardless of Iceland's firm neutrality. The *Franconia* arrives back in the Clyde on 24 May, carrying the Royal Marines, who have not, unsurprisingly, met with any armed resistance. It's a rough passage for the Marines, with heavy seas lifting the *Franconia*'s stern clear out of the water, releasing a banshee howl from her three whirling props. Luckily, that's the worst thing they have to endure on the voyage home.

 Within four days, the *Franconia* is at sea again, bound once more for the far north as part of Operation Alphabet, the Allied retreat from Norway following the success of the German invasion and the commencement of the Battle of France. She arrives at Harstad on 4 June as part of Narvik Evacuation Group I, once again with the *Lancastria* as well as four other troopships, escorted by the destroyers *Wren* and *Volunteer*. With air cover from *Ark Royal*, *Franconia* and the rest of Narvik Evacuation Group I embark 5,100 Allied troops before rendezvous at sea and the return voyage to the Clyde, convoyed by the battleship *Valiant* and her destroyer screen. On 10 June, the *Valiant* leaves the convoy to relieve Narvik Evacuation Group II, then under heavy air attack, but Group I arrives safely in Greenock without further incident. The *Franconia* is back in Liverpool by 12 June.

 So far, despite the increasing tempo of the conflict, and the ever more serious risk of submarine or air attack, the *Franconia* has gone through the war without damage from enemy fire. It's not destined to last. Barely two days after her return from Operation Alphabet, on 14 June, the *Franconia* is ordered to sea again to take part in Operation Ariel, the Allied evacuation from ports in western France, where up to 60,000 troops and civilians are thought to be waiting for rescue. On the afternoon of 16 June, she enters Quiberon Bay on the south-west coast of

Brittany, part of a flotilla of troopships and destroyers assembled to take off the Allied forces. The anchorage is subjected to intermittent German bombing and, passing through its boom defences at dead slow speed, the *Franconia* suffers two near misses from a German bomber. The engine room is plunged into darkness, and her plates ruptured. Knee deep in water, the engine room crew get the flooding under control, but the main engines have stopped and the ship's pipework has been extensively damaged. By 9.00 a.m. on 17 June, the *Franconia*'s main engines are ready for a trial restart, but an oil leak prevents any serious movement until later in the day. The *Franconia* returns to Liverpool two days later empty, but the subsequent conclusion is that only the prompt action of the engine room crew saved the ship. Her sister Cunarder, the *Lancastria*, is not so lucky: struck by German bombs on the afternoon of 17 June, she sinks within 20 minutes, with more than 3,000 dead, the greatest loss of life on board a single ship in British maritime history.

Six weeks of breakneck effort ready the *Franconia* to put to sea again, and after a brief stop at the Clyde, too painfully short for shore leave, she takes on almost 3,000 troops and heads south down the coast of West Africa. With Italy now in the war, Britain's Middle Eastern and Africa possessions are a new priority, and troops have to be shipped there despite the equally grave situation back home to protect the oil-producing territories and the Suez Canal, while avoiding the dangerous and narrow seaways of the Mediterranean and the North African coast. From end June, the "WS" convoys begin mass troop movements from the British Isles to the Middle East and India, via South and East Africa, involving some of Britain's greatest liners. By early August, the *Franconia* is ready to rejoin the war effort, and John shares the credit for the feat of seamanship that follows. With one brief stop at Freetown, she voyages safely to South Africa as part of Convoy WS 2, rounds the Cape, and sails north to her destination at Suez, travelling 12,785 miles in just six weeks. On the return journey, she carries civilian refugees from Egypt as far as Durban as part of

Convoy SW 1, taken out of harm's way now that Italy is attacking in the Middle East. Proceeding independently by the same Capetown-Freetown route, she is back in Gourock by 4 November, returning to find that the Battle of Britain has been fought and won.

The next voyage on 15 November is practically a milk run by comparison: to Gibraltar to deliver 1,370 RAF personnel for onward shipment to the eastern Mediterranean. Operation Collar, the ensuing convoy dash to Malta and Alexandria, leads to the Battle of Cape Spartivento, one of the last opportunities for the Italian fleet to inflict a significant defeat on the Royal Navy. The *Franconia*, however, is free to turn back to the Clyde, and is back in port by 14 December.

For John, that winter of 1940-41 is a last spell of home comfort in the midst of the war: frequent shore leave, his parents and sometimes his sister and her family huddled around the wireless, listening to the latest war news. After the Phoney War Christmas of 1939, it's the first true wartime Christmas, with rationing, air raid precautions and German bombing through December; Dad's even built an Anderson shelter from corrugated iron in the back garden, although when John comes back it seems to be doing double duty as a garden shed. Bizarrely, Clydebank has a boom town air to it. The John Brown Shipyard is working full out to build and repair ships; the Singer sewing machine factory has turned its production lines over to manufacturing small arms and ammunition. There's no more unemployment: jobs and wages are plentiful; family kitties and pubs are full. Most of the bombs of the Blitz have fallen further south and east; with a world at war, Clydebank seems to be leading a charmed life. Winter is bitterly cold that year, with flu rampant, but Glaswegians are used to that kind of thing.

John's bought what he could for the family at his various ports of call, and he helps to create an even brighter Christmas for them than many others in Glasgow that year. With his father, he hangs up the Christmas streamers, cut in strips from old magazines and pasted together in links like Cunard anchor chains. Even in wartime, the local fruitier has sheaves of holly branches in stock, bright with red berries. With rationing in force since mid-year, John uses his Forces' ration card, and even filches a little from ship's stores, to get the dried fruit and the golden syrup for the essential clootie dumpling. Mum dusts off the Christmas Nativity tableau and puts it under the tree – this year a small fir that John's cropped from the hedgerows by the docks. The Christmas ham is small, thanks to rationing, but at least there's plenty of clapshot and beer, as well as the rum John has brought home with him, and the wine from his shipboard wine allowance. Presents are practical – his mother's bought him a decidedly unregulation Graham tartan scarf and knitted him a pair of thick woollen socks to keep him warm on his night watches. At sea off the coast of Africa, they're the last thing he would need, but he treasures them nonetheless.

The one frustration is the ache of separation from Farah, but at least here it's less intense than in the Indian Ocean, when he has to reflect that she is just a few hundred miles away across the same sea. Her letters come more regularly too. Occasionally he wonders if he should end it and set her free, but that's just one of those perfunctory formalities of conscience, tipping his hat to accepted wisdom on the subject. He doesn't really feel it at all. For one thing she would be heartbroken if he did, but that's not the real reason. He can't envisage life or a future without her anymore. She's as much a part of his universe as the fixed stars he named for her in Arabic.

John's shore leave is soon over, though, and just after New Year, on 12 January 1941, he sets off again, bound once more for the Cape and the Middle East, ferrying a contingent of British and Australian troops as part of Convoy WS 5B of 21 merchant ships with a total tonnage of 420,000 tons, the largest convoy to date to leave the British Isles. As always, when leaving the mouth of the Clyde, he's struck by the stunning beauty of the scenery on either bank, in contrast to the bricks and soot just a little further upriver. The *Franconia* and her convoy mates pass through the boom defence near Greenock, one by one, then form into two columns until past the Mull of

Kintyre and out of the Firth of Clyde, then finally, seven columns of three ships each, with 600 yards between each ship. Two miles ahead of the merchant ships is the V-shaped destroyer screen of 12 ships, and astern of the merchant flotilla, the ageing battleship HMS *Ramillies*, and the cruisers HMS *Naiad* and *Phoebe*. The cruiser HMAS *Australia* leads the far starboard column of the convoy. Hurricanes and other RAF patrols provide air cover. It's some 4,000 miles to Freetown, the first port of call, or 20 days at sea at the convoy's expected speed of around 9 knots.

Outbound from the Clyde, the convoy steams due west, to longitude 24 degrees west, parallel with the western tip of Iceland, before turning south. As the convoy leaves submarine-infested home waters behind, the destroyer screen and other escorts drop away, following the orders of the Commander-in-Chief Western approaches, until by 17 January, the *Australia* and an old recommissioned cruiser, HMS *Emerald*, are the only two escorts left. As the weather warms, John breaks out his whites to change from his dress blues into the white tunic and shorts of the hot-weather uniform, and manages a couple of letters to Farah, filled with heartfelt feelings and short on facts. The only real alarm of this leg of the voyage, besides a silly incident when an Australian sergeant accidentally fires a Bren gun, wounding three men, comes on 19 January, with reports that a tanker, *British Union*, has been sunk by a German raider 200 miles to the south. The next day, a destroyer and Flower-class corvettes from the Freetown escort group join the convoy, and see it safely into Freetown on 25 January. At Freetown, they stay only a couple of days, and the lower ranks aren't allowed ashore for leave, but there is the usual throng of local canoes around the ships and black boys diving into the water. The *Franconia* has developed big stagnant pools of air below decks where the blackout restrictions prevent proper ventilation, and becomes a sweat bath in conditions like this. Wartime exigencies also mean they dispense with the usual ceremony of King Neptune and his court when the convoy crosses the Line, a few days out of Freetown. The convoy continues south without incident, to Cape Town, where it divides. John enjoys the cooler weather and the familiar spectacle of Table Mountain, visible from 40 miles out, ringed by the white houses and red roofs of Cape Town, but once again, there's no pause for shore leave. Some of the convoy units remain in Cape Town, while the other half, including the *Franconia*, rounds the Cape and sails onward to Durban, still escorted by the *Australia*. On 16 February the convoy arrives in Durban Harbour without a single ship lost.

John knows that Farah is close by now, just over the curve of the horizon. The four days ashore in Durban give him a chance to write to her, with a few poignant words about being so near and yet so far. He also submits his first paper to a learned journal, on early Arabic astronomical calculations of longitude, "Al-Khwarizmi's Revision of Ptolemy's Geography and the Determination of Indian Ocean Coordinates." It's hardly the kind of thing the rest of the ship's complement are exactly conversant with. The troops are given shore leave for the first time in a month, and behave well on the whole, although there are plenty of drunks staggering up the gangplanks, and a few posted AWOL who overstay their time ashore and only get back on board at the last minute. The convoy's departure is supposed to be secret, but a crowd of onlookers, including many pretty girls in slacks and shorts, assemble to see her off, with a chorus of the "Maori Farewell" from the Australian troops.

The *Franconia* and other convoy elements continue their northward journey through the Mozambique Channel. As the weather warms again, more and more of the troops come out to sleep on deck. Training drills, lectures and courses keep the men busy: with his scientific bent, John takes an interest in one, on the optics of rangefinding and sniping, and joins in rifle drill, brushing up on his basic RNVR training and scoring well. The *Franconia*'s card room is turned into a court by the Australian command, and various offenders, including the latecomers at Durban, put on trial and sentenced. The sergeant who fired the Bren is exonerated.

On the night of 27 February, they reach one of the most dangerous stages of the voyage, the passage through the Straits of Bab El Mandeb, only 17 miles wide and too narrow for useful evasion if a German bomber comes over. Captain Taunton insists on the strictest blackout precautions and posts extra lookouts. John is on watch that night, and keeps his eyes peeled, peering into the dark until first light dawns and the hawsers and masts are outlined against the sky. They finally drop anchor off Port Tewfik on 4 March, where they find that the Suez Canal is too heavily mined to proceed further for the planned docking at Alexandria for final disembarkation of the troops. Instead, the troops are put ashore at Suez. John takes advantage of the delay to brush up on his basic Arabic for his astronomical studies. By mid-March, he is back at Aden at the southern end of the Red Sea when news reaches him of the Clydebank Blitz.

Chapter 12

Cole returns to his full creative form in 1938 with *Leave It to Me!*, a show ironically based on a hit play about Stalinist Russia. After tryouts in New Haven and Boston, the musical opens on 9 November at the Imperial Theatre, and is an instant hit, running for 291 performances, with a return engagement in September 1939 for 16 more. One critic hails Cole's contributions as "among his best, sounding newer and neater than anything he has done in several years." For the secondary role of a gold-digging adventuress, Cole auditions a young ingenue, Mary Martin, in his New York apartment, and is so struck by her performance that he insists at once that "this is the girl." Mary Martin makes her Broadway debut in the show, singing "My Heart Belongs to Daddy," instantly creating a mini-legend of her own. By December, she is the cover girl for *Life*. "Along comes Mary Martin, and overnight the dingus becomes better known than the name of the show in which it is sung," Cole comments soon after, in an interview with the *New York Herald Tribune*. In the same interview, Cole also declares that: "one really big hit song is all any show should have," but unfortunately, "nobody can, with any degree of consistent accuracy, tell what is going to catch the public ear and be a hit song. I certainly can't." He does at least pay tribute to Artie Shaw and his version of "Begin the Beguine," which "wasn't a tenth the hit it is at this very moment." Gene Kelly also makes his first Broadway appearance in the show, as an ensemble dancer, landing the job of holding Mary Martin while she sings her famous number. In its original Broadway incarnation, *Leave It to Me!* also features Joseph Stalin, who leads a final dance to "The Internationale." After the signing of the Molotov–Ribbentrop Pact in August 1939, Stalin is dropped from the return engagement.

The darkening global situation impinges on Cole's life in other ways. In 1939, Linda closes their Paris home and moves many of its furnishings to a newly purchased country retreat in the Berkshire mountains, near Williamstown, Massachusetts.

It's a sprawling estate, with a large low-lying main house and separate cottage, and Linda quickly remodels it to their taste, converting a barn to a garage with guest apartment en suite. Cole takes to using the gatekeeper's cottage as his private creative studio, putting up a "No Trespassing" sign when he's engrossed in work. He keeps up his creative pace, and his next show, *Du Barry Was a Lady*, opening on 6 December 1939 at the 46th Street Theatre and transferring to the Royale Theatre in October 1940, runs for 406 performances. Its bizarre yet burlesque-tinged plot, involving Ethel Merman and Bert Lahr, who's just won immortality earlier that year as the Cowardly Lion in *The Wizard of Oz*, in a dream excursion to the court of Louis XV, catches the eye of the Boston censors during its pre-Broadway tryouts and other prudish critics such as Brooks Atkinson, and some of its songs are banned from airplay. Others, though, like "Do I Love You" and "Well, Did You Evah," become classics. "Miss Merman is the perfect musical comedy minstrel," enthuses the *New York Times*. Betty Grable gets her first big break with a role in the show, and is whisked away to Hollywood the following year to become World War 2's top pinup girl and one of the biggest stars of the Forties. Gossip soon links her name with Artie Shaw.

By 1940, Cole has settled down into a consistent working routine at his New York headquarters, a three-room suite on the 41st floor of the Waldorf Towers, where his secretary and valet keep the world at bay, fielding calls and callers, handling the necessary business contacts with agents, arrangers, managers and producers. Cole's workplace is his living room, equipped with a grand piano, a radio phonograph, a card table with drinks and a cocktail shaker, and stacks of records and dictionaries. Linda has her own apartment just across the way. At the piano, Cole roughs out the running order of a show on charts to judge and vary the pacing, fuelled by cigarettes and throat tablets. A waiter, permanently assigned to him, brings him his light lunches. He usually avoids setting fingers to keys until he has already worked out the words and music in his head and written them down, before running through them at the keyboard. His injuries have not impaired his playing, nor his singing. During rehearsals for new shows, he often drills the cast rigorously on the correct pronunciation and intonation of his songs.

Cole's next big hit, *Panama Hattie,* another Merman vehicle all about ships, spies and saboteurs in the Panama Canal Zone, is an even bigger success than *Du Barry Was a Lady* and his longest running show so far, opening at the 46th Street Theatre on 30 October 1940, and running until January 1942, with 501 performances. "Cole Porter wrote the music and lyrics in his pithiest style, and Ethel Merman sings them like a high-compression engine," declares Brooks Atkinson's *New York Times* review. "Cole plus Merman is a combination that has yielded some memorable musical shows in recent years." In fact, her stage presence has a lot to do with the success of the show; even though the *New York Herald Tribune* proclaims that the score is "filled with any number of excellent songs," none of them prove enduring hits. It also inaugurates a run of highly popular yet creatively stale shows throughout the early Forties, probably successful because of wartime America's hunger for entertainment as much as any other reason. Cole still enjoys the rewards, however, wining and dining out with his valet to lean on, and continues to attend his own first nights with a glittering lineup of friends.

It's not all song and dance for Cole, though. His leg injuries continue to torment him, and he undergoes a series of ultimately abortive surgical procedures to try to lessen the damage. In one typical operation of the period, the surgeon begins by rebreaking his femurs, removing the jagged ends of bone, splicing Cole's Achilles tendons, and removing eight inches from his tibias for bone grafts over the damage sites. Osteomyelitis is one of the most persistent and intractable infections known, and Cole has it in full force. The staphylococcal infections that complicated the original fractures have never entirely died away, and continue to interfere with healing, and compound the agony from persistent nerve damage and scarring.

Chapter 13

Artie spends three months in Acapulco. He claims to have broken his leg during his stay, attempting to rescue a woman bather who was being dragged out to sea by the undertow. That's the end of his Mexican stay, but he returns to the US with a song in mind.

While in Acapulco, Artie hears "Frenesi" by Mexican songwriter Alberto Domínguez, originally composed for the marimba. Back in Hollywood, he records his own version in March 1940 with a studio band, adding woodwinds, French horns and a string section along to the usual dance band lineup for almost the first time in jazz history, producing another instant hit. Artie's excursion to Mexico hasn't voided his recording contract either, or the corresponding royalties. *Radio and Television Mirror* praises the "sincerity and honesty" that led him to his decision, his refusal "to accept the true with the false, the gold with the dross." The fact is, though, that Artie is back to play music, and music as commercial – and successful – as any he's yet recorded.

First appearing on the *Billboard* pop charts in August, "Frenesi" reaches Number One by 21 December 1940, and stays there for 13 weeks. It becomes one of the biggest single hits of the entire 1940s, later joining the Grammy Hall of Fame. Big string sections, with violins, violas and cellos, become part of his established repertoire, rising to a full 32-piece orchestra, giving him the range to take his music away from dance hits towards more melodic pieces. *Victor Record Review* in April quotes Artie stating that "The general idea… is not to get away from swing music but to present dance music with more color and variety than is possible with the usual brass and saxophone setup that has perhaps, due to constant usage, become monotonous."

Artie has more immediate issues on hand, though; Betty Grable not being one of them. He renews contact with Lana Turner, his co-star in *Dancing Co-Ed*, and in February 1940 she elopes with him to Las Vegas. In March, they take a honeymoon trip to New York, to introduce Lana to Artie's childhood home, staying in luxury hotels, taking in Broadway shows, and touring the city's best live music venues, to listen and to dance. At the Ice Terrace Room of the New Yorker Hotel, dancing to Bob Crosby's band, Artie hears the brilliant young trumpeter Billy Butterfield, and arranges for him to join his band on the West Coast. Butterfield ends up staying with Artie longer than Lana Turner does: the marriage lasts just four months. Shortly after the divorce is granted in September 1940, Lana Turner discovers that she is pregnant with Artie's child, and has an abortion.

From July, Artie resumes regular radio work, providing music and other turns for NBC Studios' "The Burns and Allen Show," with George Burns and Gracie Allen. In August, he starts filming with Fred Astaire and Paulette Goddard for *Second Chorus*, a Hollywood musical comedy. As a film, it's not much, aside from some fine footwork by Fred Astaire, seen at one point conducting Artie's orchestra. Astaire later dubs it the worst film he ever made. It does inspire Artie to write his "Concerto for Clarinet," one of his best pieces, described by one critic as "Artie's masterpiece to date," even though he later claims it was just filler music for the movie. He also contributes "Love of My Life" with Johnny Mercer, which Astaire sings to Paulette Goddard. That nets Artie an Oscar nomination for Best Song. And in Fred Astaire, at least he meets a fellow artist he can respect. Artie later characterizes him as "a humorless Teutonic man, the opposite of his debonair image in top hat and tails," but one who sweats and toils, rehearsing 12 hours a day, seven days a week, with the same dedication to perfection that Artie brings to his music.

Artie resists pressure to take his new orchestra on the road, perhaps learning from his experiences of the past couple of years. It's about this time that Artie forms his Gramercy Five, a smaller unit within his larger orchestra, named after his old area telephone exchange in New York and including, of all things, a harpsichord in its lineup, played by Johnny Guarnieri. It's a not unusual pattern at the time, undertaken by Benny Goodman among others, and the Gramercy Five numbers a couple of former Goodman bandsmen. Billy Butterfield plays trumpet, with Al Hendrickson on guitar, Nick Fatool on drums, and Jack DeNaut on bass. With the Gramercy Five, Artie records eight records from September 1940 to early 1941, including "Summit Ridge Drive," another million-selling hit. He achieves similar feats with his full orchestra, though, recording a legendary version of Hoagy Carmichael's "Star Dust" in October, with Billy Butterfield on trumpet and Jack Jenny on trombone, the three scintillating soloists reaching unheard-of heights with their instruments, framed by the full lush backdrop of the Orchestra's horns and strings. After that, his band is christened the Star Dust Band.

In February 1941, Artie signs a new contract with RCA, also recording a superb double-side of "Dancing In the Dark" and "Smoke Gets in Your Eyes," featuring the full Orchestra for the dance number and the Gramercy Five for the B-side. *Variety* calls the A-side "one of the best sides Shaw has ever made." By late March, *Variety* is also reporting that Artie plans only to record in future, rather than tour or perform live, and to go searching the American backwoods in quest of genuine traditional American music, to record with ensembles of various sizes. By April, he's reportedly retired into seclusion in New York, studying classical music with Dr Hans Byrns, an Austrian refugee and former director of the Vienna State Opera, and touring Manhattan nightspots with date after date, the plans to study ethnic American music on hold. At this point, the Gramercy Five and the Star Dust Band are essentially defunct, although Artie has one more superlative release with them in May, a disc of "My Blue Heaven" with the Gramercy Five, coupled with "Moonglow" by the full orchestra.

Artie concludes his last obligations under his previous recording contract in June with some studio work backed by session musicians, freeing him up to indulge some more creative autonomy. He then decides to assemble yet another band, his biggest to date, conceived with a definite eye towards touring, with a female vocalist and 32 musicians, including the brilliant black trumpeter and singer Oran "Hot Lips" Page. The lineup has five sax players, three trombones, four trumpets, four rhythm players, and 15 string players, who Artie dubs "the mice." His managers call the new outfit Artie Shaw and His Symphonic Swing, although it still appears as Artie Shaw and His Orchestra in the discs of the time: "Symphonic" anyway is more about the heavy string emphasis than the style of music.

In September 1941, *Down Beat* reports on Artie intensively rehearsing his new band in Manhattan's Nola Studios for up to eight hours a day: "When Artie asks for something, he gets it." Artie records six sides early that month with his new band, including a version of the title song of the just-released film noir musical *Blues in the Night*. Record companies at the time make no bones about releasing competing versions of popular new numbers, and Artie's version becomes a classic, showcasing Page. On 6 September, Artie leads his band out onto the stage at the Marine Ballroom on the Steel Pier at Atlantic City, New Jersey, his first appearance at a major East Coast venue since his flight to Mexico in November 1939. Anchored by the superlative jazz drummer David Tough, the new ensemble is a highly disciplined and immensely powerful outfit, able to deliver swing as well as consistency. Artie follows up with a tour of most eastern states, with a detour into Canada. Fans are as avid as ever for Artie, and mob his tour buses for autographs at every stop. The Mice often travel in a separate coach. After 27 September, though, Artie cancels over 30 tour dates because venues in the South have objected to putting Hot Lips Page onstage. With a reshuffled itinerary in the Midwest, Artie and his band wind up in Chicago by 30 October for another Victor recording session, and continue touring into November, crossing the country in the same caravan arrangement. This time, Artie seems to be surviving, even thriving, under the strain of touring.

The next break in Artie's career doesn't come from his mercurial temperament. He's playing a theatre in Rhode Island with his orchestra when the news comes over the radio that the Japanese have bombed Pearl Harbor.

Chapter 14

John receives the news of the death of his parents and his sister by official Admiralty telegraph message a few days after the actual bombing on 13 and 14 March 1941: *Deeply regret to inform you that your father lost his life as result of enemy action.*

John is privileged in one way: as an employee of the dockyard, his father has received an official card for notification of next of kin, to be carried inside his National Registration identity booklet. The card has somehow survived the bomb blast that killed John's parents and destroyed the family home, and the Admiralty machinery has clicked into gear and sent the notification of decease. It's about all that does work properly during and after the Clydebank Blitz.

The new German bombing offensive from early March 1941 has already provided ample advance warning, with attacks on other cities. Isolated reconnaissance flights over Clydebank give even more advance warning of what's to come. Clydebank is an obvious military target. The Admiralty oil depot at its western limits; the Royal Ordnance Factory at Dalmuir; the Beardmore and John Brown shipyards filling the northern riverbank between them; the sprawling Singer works just inland, surrounded by smaller factories, docks and railway lines: it's a bomber's dream of a target-rich environment. The 12,000 homes and 55,000 people in the immediate vicinity are almost an afterthought in comparison. Local officials have made few preparations for an attack, believing they are a low priority. And with the population's vital role in war work in the factories close by, evacuation is out of the question.

The night of 13 March 1941 sees a bomber's moon over Clydebank, a full moon in a clear sky. The German bombers approach from the direction of Loch Lomond to the north-west, to avoid radar detection and flak. In the event, they needn't have worried. Around 7:30 p.m., British military intelligence sends a warning to Glasgow and Clydebank that an attack might be imminent, based on the bearing of German radio

93

direction-finding beams, but the warning is ignored. The German pathfinders, fresh from devastating Coventry four months before, have no problem picking out their target. A yellow alarm of a possible air raid is received by phone at the Bankhead School A.F.S. Watch Room at 8:30 p.m., followed shortly after by a purple alarm, indicating a probable attack. At around 9:00 p.m. the air raid sirens sound; many residents ignore them, expecting another false alarm. Some of the first bombs hit the Yoker Distillery, lighting a beacon of burning whisky for the ensuing waves of bombers to follow: it's soon joined by the Singer timber yards and the first of the Admiralty oil depots. High explosives and incendiaries rain down on the town, catching hundreds of people in the cramped closes and shelters. Entire streets are blown down by parachute mines; John's beloved Central Library takes a direct hit. The Bankhead School A.F.S. Watch Room, nerve centre for the local civil defence, suffers another direct hit from a parachute mine just 15 minutes after the raid begins, with 39 dead.

Clydebank burns so fiercely that the light can be seen from Northern Ireland. Fire engines and ambulances are called in from central Glasgow to help out the overwhelmed local services, ferrying the wounded to hospital, leaving the dead where they lie, but as the fires and devastation worsen, road access into and out of Clydebank is blocked. The Locharbriggs red sandstone, characteristic of the region, proves a horribly effective obstacle, once blown into the streets to create impromptu barricades. Phone lines are cut, and central coordination of rescue and relief breaks down. Just 45 minutes after the commencement of the raid, Dalmuir has lost all water, electricity and phone connections. The streets stink of burning flesh.

The RAF's defensive plan, Operation Fighternight, a recent innovation, proves a complete failure. Spitfires of No. 602 Squadron, originally a local Royal Auxiliary Air Force unit with ties to the community, patrolling at 20,000 feet, are denied permission to descend and engage for fear of exposing them to anti-aircraft fire lower down. In the event, the German bombers only report appreciable AA fire 35 minutes after the raid begins. The four AA guns allocated to defend Clydebank, supposed to drive the waves of bombers up to higher altitude, are powerless against the attackers, and run out of ammunition around 10:50 p.m. The Polish destroyer ORP *Piorun*, originally built by John Brown before her sale to Poland, and under repair in the John Brown shipyards, keeps up a gallant but futile AA fire against the German bombers. Their efforts notwithstanding, the Germans are able to drop some 400 tons of explosives and 500 tons of incendiaries onto Clydebank without any appreciable opposition. Operation Fighternight is retired after the first night of the Clydebank Blitz.

The last German bomb falls on Clydebank at around 5:30 a.m., and the "all clear" sounds an hour later, just before dawn. The morning of 14 March reveals acres of rubble with a few walls and shells of houses left standing in surreal isolation. An exodus of refugees on foot begins immediately, despite the rubble roadblocks. Those who stay behind mostly await organized evacuation, in vain: communications are still down and no one knows where the groups of survivors are. The second night of bombing begins at 8:40 p.m., with almost as many bombers as on the first.

John never finds out exactly what happened to his family. His father's body, pulled from under a rubble pile yards from the family house, is one of the more recognizable corpses. Other bodies are just lost in the chaos of the mortuaries, and subsequently shovelled together into the ground in mass burials – his mother, his sister, her husband and their four children presumably among them. The authorities can't even provide enough cardboard coffins for all the dead, many of whom are laid to rest in knotted bedsheets. Some shelters take direct hits and are never exhumed, just filled in afterwards with the fragments of bodies inside. Only 2,000 people remain. Only eight houses out of the 12,000 are undamaged; two thirds are either totally destroyed or left uninhabitable. Clydebank is the only British town in the entire war to be evacuated.

By comparison, the military targets have gotten off lightly.

Only one fifth of the Admiralty oil tanks are hit; the John Brown shipyards are barely affected; the Singer plant has lost a lot of burned wood and some damaged offices, but war production resumes within weeks.

The authorities clamp down on any mention of the scale of the disaster. On 18 March 1941 the Ministry of Home Security issues an official communiqué stating that "about 500 persons had been killed in the raids in Clydeside." The *Glasgow Herald* rhapsodizes over the "cool, unwavering courage of the people." Later official death totals rise to 528; the actual figure is likely at least double.

When John returns to Clydebank on 21 May, he has no idea what to expect. As the *Franconia* sails up the Clyde, the dockyards, though showing some damage, are mostly back in working order and show very little scarring. Aside from the notice of bereavement, and a few scattered hints on the wireless, he's not come across any full account of the bombing, or the damage done. There are hints in the prospect beyond the docks, but the familiar landmarks, the Titan crane and the Singer factory clock tower, are still there unscathed. It's only when he steps ashore for his shore leave that he realizes what has happened. He finds a ghost town, a moonscape where workers are still only starting to clear away the worst of the debris. The smell of crushed and destroyed homes is almost as bad as the occasional tang of decay from beneath mounds of stone. The registry in the town centre confirms the news he already had about his family. His other brothers are still serving and unable to join him. Occasionally he runs across a familiar neighbour or family friend of old, but he can't find a single living relative in his home town. He can't break through the wall of numbness to feel his full grief because of the total devastation around him. It's as if the human world he knew has simply been erased, wiped clean away, and a few last, doomed survivors are still hanging on in the resulting void. The shipyard cranes loom like scavenging storks above the carnage. Individual human loss almost feels irrelevant in this total annihilation.

John can find nothing in the newspaper and wireless reports to reflect the scale of the disaster. There are the usual reasons for the secrecy and censorship – and some not so usual. The authorities naturally fear that the extent of the damage at Clydebank, and the success (or not) of the air raid could be valuable intelligence for the enemy, and should not be told. After all, the last thing anyone wants is a return raid to finish the job. Then there's the fiasco of the RAF response to the raids, and the treatment of the residents afterwards. That doesn't reflect much credit on the Scottish Office, or many others in authority. There's also official concern over the spectre of Scottish nationalism, and finally, anxiety in Whitehall about the legacy of Red Clydeside and the strong local socialist tradition. In those days before Operation Barbarossa and the end of the Nazi-Soviet Pact, there are still some misgivings about potential Bolshevik subversion, and the events in Clydebank would be meat for agitation.

John isn't to know any of this. He is quietly enraged at the wall of silence and obfuscation, though. As a rational and patriotic serviceman, he can see the arguments in favour of it; but he can't swallow it in relation to what he's seen, and what's happened to his family. He can't direct his anger openly against his superiors and his government; and yet it festers, unappeased. The official obscurantism and deception compounds the usual bafflement of bereavement, the exasperation at the randomness of fate, and frustrates his grief still further. Normally a quiet, diffident type, he becomes a grim, brooding one, the cliched Caledonian stoicism masking the turmoil within. His rage, denied an outlet, transfers its focus to the Germans and other enemy forces. Even if he felt able to mourn, he hardly has time to. He's snatched away on 3 June, for another swift convoy run to Durban, this time returning mercifully to Liverpool by mid-August. In the interim, Nazi Germany invades the Soviet Union, and the war suddenly takes on a very different complexion.

John does have time to write to Farah, telling her the news in a few laconic paragraphs, hating himself for the self-censorship he's performed to make sure that the message reaches her, leaving out all the details on the destruction of Clydebank. She writes back, tenderly, in a letter that he receives a few weeks later:

Darling, I'm so so sorry to hear of your loss. Your parents were the loveliest, kindest people. And their home as well was so nice. Everyone says these things happen in war, but it's still so evil, and it seems like it takes only the best. May God keep them. And may He watch over you, my love. Stay safe for me.

That dreadful numbness creeps over him again when he reads her words. Will he ever be able to feel properly, ever be able to love her as he did? Right now, the only emotions that feel remotely real are anger and hate. For six dreary weeks in August and September 1941, he kills time in Liverpool, not daring to return home when there is no home to return to. He never took the shipboard boxing matches seriously in peacetime; now he finds the *Franconia*'s most prized pugilist, a grizzled stoker, and learns how to box. He resumes Merchant Navy rifle drill and scores top marks. His high scores are easily explained: he just imagines a German face on every target. His only respite from the treadmill of rage and aggression is his mathematical and astronomical studies, when he can lose himself among the stars, in the cool blue oceans between the constellations. The compliments and letters of praise on his learned paper are so much cold comfort, although he does try to take the time to answer them in the journals. It's only the pure clear spaces of mathematics and astronomy that grant him solace. Brief hours of prayer under the unfinished vaults of Giles Gilbert Scott's great Anglican cathedral are no help: its red Woolton sandstone reminds him too much of Clydebank.

John soon reaches a resolution about what to do with his anger. By end September, though, the *Franconia* has set sail again, once more for Africa and the Middle East, this time as part of Convoy WS 12 to reinforce air defences around the Iraqi oil fields and other key strongpoints in the Middle East. It's another major convoy of 24 merchant vessels, escorted by a changing cast of cruisers, destroyers, armed merchant cruisers, battlecruisers, battleships, corvettes and one aircraft carrier, HMS *Argus*. John's freedom to act on his resolution is severely circumscribed. The Emergency Work (Merchant Navy) Order, passed in early May just before John's return to the Clyde, has changed his terms of service. Now, instead of being a volunteer free to transfer to other branches of service, he is required to serve in the Merchant Marine for the duration of the war. Any application for a transfer becomes a much more difficult and laborious procedure. John decides to try anyway. There follows an odd, stilted interview with Captain Bisset.

"I want to undertake more active service, Sir."

"Do you mean you want to transfer off the ship? To join the regular Navy? I can't really spare any senior men right now, Graham; especially a gifted navigator like yourself. And I must say, I think you undervalue our work here if you feel you would be helping the war effort more under the White Ensign. Giving thousands of our boys safe passage matters more than killing a few Jerries. We keep the arteries of war flowing, man. Look at the work we did in Norway, in France. I don't need to tell you how vital that is."

"It's not that, Sir," Graham continues clumsily. "I just would like to have more of a crack at them: you know, strike a blow myself against the enemy. I've learned how to fight, and shoot, Sir. I can do my part."

"You lost your parents in the Blitz, didn't you, Graham?" the Captain asks sharply.

Still at attention, staring straight ahead, Graham flinches. "Yes, Sir," he manages finally.

"I can understand the wish to get some of your own back," the Captain responds, somewhat more sympathetically. "God knows there are enough who would like that. Look, here's what I'll do. I understand we may be more in the front line soon. I'll recommend you for appropriate training and any opportunity that comes up. Just hold off on any transfer request until then, will you? There's a good fellow."

John's wishes are more or less academic anyway while the ship is still at sea. After arrival at Aden on 20 November, the convoy disperses and each ship proceeds to Suez independently. He finds the smattering of Arabic he has picked up from astronomy surprisingly useful, and devotes spare time to more language study, attempting to master it with small talk in the streets and bazaars of Port Tewfik. Then suddenly he gets his wish. The Captain calls him to his cabin for an audience with a gritty-looking Army officer who seems to have desert sand ground into his tanned skin and his rather tatty khakis. On his desk is a map, which appears to be of the North African desert, and atop it, a Colt automatic.

"This is Captain MacAlistair of the Long Range Desert Group," the Captain introduces the lean Army officer. "He has been looking around for an expert in celestial navigation who knows some Arabic, to assist with a long-range reconnaissance patrol into the desert. After your recent request, I thought you might be interested."

John nods mutely. It's the last thing he had been expecting. The Army officer steps forward and extends a sunburned hand.

"A pleasure to meet you, laddie," he says, without a trace of a Scottish accent, despite his name. "Glaswegian, I understand? And you can shoot as well, I hear. Good. Can I interest you in a little job of sneak thievery?"

"Um, absolutely, Sir," John stammers, returning the man's hard handshake.

Captain MacAlistair explains the mission, as far as he can when he is unable to name locations. His patrol needs help to reconnoitre positions behind enemy lines, in desert areas where there are no landmarks and the only navigation is by the stars. "We can't use standard prismatic compasses near tanks and trucks, so we rely on the sun and the stars. Something you sailor chappies are good at." The patrol's last navigator "met with a wee accident," the Captain explains, and they need a replacement to stay on schedule. "Time is pressing," Captain MacAlistair divulges. "But we'll have you back to your ship in a jiffy, before you sail again. Just a few days in the desert."

John jumps at the chance. Fate seems to have served up just what he wanted, on a plate. He isn't offered the Colt: he wonders if the Captain intended it as a signal or a piece of theatre. Instead, they issue him with a set of Army khakis, and pack him on a Waco Series C biplane for a flight west: John's first flight in a plane. Captain MacAlistair explains the mission to him during the flight, pulling out a creased map to outline the route.

"We need to scout south and west of the Qattara Depression," he reveals. "I'm sure you heard that we have a bit of a scrap going on along the coast. Our job is to reconnoitre along the Libyan border further south, and make sure that the Eyeties and Jerries aren't trying to turn our lines or slip something past us. Fast in, fast out, no contact, that's the idea. Just like slipping out of bounds after lights-out."

At this point, John starts to have misgivings. Not because of the navigational chores, which seem simple enough, even in the desert; nor because of the risks of scouting around enemy positions. No, it's the gleam of enthusiasm in MacAlistair's eye, the schoolboy eagerness to play some little prank. John can't trust that attitude to war, not after what he's already witnessed in Norway and France, and Clydebank. Besides, he volunteered for this assignment to have a chance to kill Germans, and now he's being told that the mission priority is not to even shoot at any Germans. Still, it's a little too late to raise that perfectly reasonable objection.

The Waco touches down at Siwa Oasis, a surprisingly verdant and built-up area after all the warnings of trackless desert. "Even the palms seem to be swaying," John thinks briefly, recalling the lyrics of the song, and dancing with Farah, but these definitely aren't the palms of the Seychelles. He's introduced to the rest of the patrol, most of them wearing wool caps and even more grubby khakis than their captain; and is shown round the patrol vehicles: a CMP Ford 15 cwt truck for MacAlistair, and six CMP Ford 30 cwt trucks, one of them mounting a Bofors 37 mm anti-tank gun behind an armoured gun shield. To John's eyes, the vehicles look more like go-karts than actual trucks, stripped down almost to their bare chassis, and showing more blankets and tarpaulins than bodywork.

"We just took back this oasis a couple of weeks ago," MacAlistair explains, as they sit down to a basic meal of Army field rations round the campfire. "We need to probe west into the Great Sand Sea to see if the Italians aren't planning a return match to draw off pressure from further north. It lives up to its name out there, believe me, waves and all. That's where you can help out."

After a fly-infested night under canvas, they set out the next morning before dawn, to get as much driving done as they can across the miles of flat gravel country fringing the Great Sand Sea before the full heat of the day. They make good time, and John wonders if there was really any point bringing him along. He's been given a .303 rifle, but with strict instructions not to use it unless ordered. He thinks again once they reach the true sandy desert. The Great Sand Sea has its waves sure enough: razorback dunes up to 300 feet high, often a mile between the crests of one dune line and the next, soft and steep-sided, especially on the eastern side. Surmounting them requires the driver to accelerate towards the crest up a slope sometimes as steep as one in three, then slow as the truck goes over the top, and surf down the gentler western slope into the trough between dunes, keeping the wheels straight to prevent the vehicle toppling over. At the crest of each dune, John can see nothing but more and more sand, in every direction, under a fierce and changeless desert sky. The enormous, empty solitude is even more impressive than midocean, walled off from the rest of the world by mile upon mile of featureless sand. Memories of T.E. Lawrence's *Revolt in the Desert* start to creep back into his mind.

John sits all day in the navigating truck beside the driver, watching the sun compass and the speedometer, a watch in his hand as he logs the distance travelled. He finds the sun compass surprisingly functional. It's like a sundial, with a tall needle-like gnomon and the kind of numbered base that recalls stone plinths in country gardens. He consults the azimuth tables to find the sun's azimuth for the time of day, and has no trouble keeping the patrol on course. The other men are very self-sufficient, evidently completely confident in their respective jobs, and do not disturb him so long as he is doing his. At every halt, once the trucks' endless jolting has stopped, he double-checks his calculations with a sextant. There would be no chance in a sandstorm, he knows, but the sky stays clear and changeless over the hundreds of miles of their journey. At sunset, they camp in flatter areas, with their tyre tracks snaking to their stopping point across the otherwise unmarked sand. Then John pulls out his theodolite and starts taking the sightings of the stars, brilliant and unclouded in the desert sky, reading the Astronomical Navigation Tables by the glow of the wireless operator's inspection lamp. John starts to form speculations about how the Arabs developed such a strong aptitude for astronomy and celestial navigation. He also gets the worst of the nighttime cold, when the temperature drops like a stone, and crawls into his blanket to shiver underneath his truck.

After days of bouncing, bruising desert driving, they reach their destination: a trail through a wadi in a slightly flatter, less sandy stretch of desert, with even one or two microscopic scrubs poking through the gravel. MacAlistair positions them in the dunes overlooking the trail.

"It's an old slave road," he chuckles salaciously. "We'll stake it out and see if there's any movement along it. If not, we move further west, and so on until we see any signs of enemy activity."

For two nights, they lie in wait with binoculars and telescopic sights trained on the trail. They see nothing, except for a Bedouin patrol far off down the road. John finds this inaction even more intensely frustrating, although the men of the LRDG seem habituated to it, and hardly move during the day, once they've found or made themselves a suitable patch of shade. He can't help casting a covetous eye towards those tempting-looking Lewis guns and Brownings mounted on the trucks. At least at night he can enjoy the brilliant vault of the stars, like the shining mosaics on the dome of a mosque, and make notes for his own pleasure. On the second day, a single distant plane flies over to the west, too far away to make out the type or nationality.

"It's probably Italian," MacAlistair confides. "Nothing to worry about, really. They can hardly see you even when they're directly overhead, so long as you don't move about and leave a trail."

All the same, next day MacAlistair decides on a move further to the west. The unit breaks camp, leaving their previous positions, and heads further down the trail. They don't get far. Sliding down the western face of a dune, leading the patrol, MacAlistair's truck ploughs into a mine, which flips the front of the vehicle up into the air in a plume of sand. When the dust has settled, they find that MacAlistair's driver has had his head blown off by the blast. MacAlistair himself has somehow avoided more than flesh wounds on his upper body, but a chunk of shrapnel has torn up his right thigh.

"Fuck," he swears, covered in his own blood and the blood of the dead driver. They pull him out of the truck, and the medical orderly bandages his leg and shoots him full of morphine. The truck itself is clearly inoperable, and after dividing its essential stores among the other vehicles, the lieutenant acting as MacAlistair's second-in-command decides that the mission needs to be aborted. They set a demolition charge in the ruined truck, and the explosion far behind them as they head back east is the loudest that John hears during the entire excursion. MacAlistair lies on a stretcher in the back of John's truck on the return journey, swearing almost continuously, his eyes red with pain and fatigue, and the blood soaking through the bandage on his thigh, dried in irregular dark patches. On the next night after the explosion, the patrol's radio man calls in an air evacuation for MacAlistair, which arrives the following day on a flat patch of desert perfect for an impromptu landing ground. John catches the same Waco biplane with MacAlistair back to Cairo. By this time, MacAlistair is delirious, with a nurse leaning over him the entire flight. At Cairo, an ambulance whisks him away, and a staff car collects John for a quick debriefing. The LRDG evidently have no more use for him, and he's back on board the *Franconia* in time for Christmas.

Much has changed in those few weeks, with the news in December that the Japanese have attacked Pearl Harbor, followed by the German and Italian declarations of war against the US and America's entry into the war on the Allied side. To the west, the new Eighth Army has launched Operation Crusader to relieve Tobruk and safeguard the Suez Canal, fielding 118,000 men and some 740 tanks. John realizes that he's in a different, much more dynamic war, with the balance shifting week by week. There's to be no talk of transfers and new assignments. On the way back westward, they stop at Mombasa, and before their return home comes the news of the fall of Singapore on 15 February. A few days after, the *Franconia* is back in the Clyde, but with only a few days of shore leave allowed. Captain Bisset is transferred to a new command, the RMS *Queen Mary*, and replaced by Captain Bertenshaw. John is about to get the taste of battle he wanted. The *Franconia* is set to depart as part of Convoy WS 17, for Operation Ironclad and the invasion of Madagascar.

Chapter 15

John spends a couple of intensely lonely weeks on Clydeside in February and March 1942. He stays in one of the University halls of residence left unoccupied by the departure of students for the war effort, not daring to take lodgings in Clydebank, but surrounded by memories of Farah. He takes a single melancholy trip west to find the town still almost as desolate as before. The town council has started reconstruction of some houses: a bare couple of hundred against the thousands needed. The Scottish Department has refused to authorize more, he's told, due to some regulation that prohibits local councils from spending more on the reconstruction of houses than their final value. He pays a brief visit to the common grave of the dead and leaves flowers there, then catches the train back east. Kelvingrove in wartime is bleak in the cold spring weather, with scattered sandbagged emplacements and the occasional bomb crater. The University halls are poorly heated thanks to coal rationing, and John endures unpleasant reminders of desert nights. He thinks of Farah walking in those courts, and writes her a brief, desultory letter. It's almost a relief to end his leave and get back on shipboard.

John's next convoy, WS 17, is bound for India, with the *Franconia* carrying units of the 13th Brigade Group of the 5th Division, destined for Bombay. Events take a different turn after departure, though. The fall of Singapore in February, Japanese occupation of the Andaman Islands on 23 March – the same day that John sets sail from the Clyde – and the first Japanese sorties against Ceylon in March and early April convince the British Chiefs of Staff that a major Japanese offensive across the Indian Ocean is imminent. Madagascar, then still under the nominal authority of the Vichy French government, presents a grave strategic challenge: Japanese submarines and warships based there could disrupt Allied supply lines to the Middle East, India and Australasia intolerably. Diego Suarez at the north end of the island is the third largest natural harbour in the world. The French port facilities there at Antsiranana are the size of Scapa Flow, with ten miles of quays and docks, a great jetty protecting the harbour entrance, and a dry dock big enough to take a battleship. Furthermore, British diplomatic circles conclude that the Vichy leadership on Madagascar is well-organized, disciplined and very loyal to Vichy ideals. The War Office has already been fostering the SOE espionage operation inside Madagascar since November the previous year, and has firm intelligence on the situation there. Churchill decides that British forces have to seize the island.

Planning begins in earnest in mid-March. This is Britain's first amphibious assault since the disaster in the Dardanelles during World War 1, and one conducted at very long range. The British high command has decided to exclude the Free French, after the failed joint attempt to occupy Dakar in September 1940, relying only on Imperial forces. With such an urgent matter in hand, it's easiest to merge Convoy WS17, already under way, into the operational plans. Despite bitter complaints from India, the forces are diverted as additional reserves for the assault. The full force assembled for Operation Ironclad is the largest since Gallipoli.

Gallipoli is not a good precedent, and the planners are eager to avoid it. A direct frontal attack on the harbour at Diego Suarez, with its heavy coastal batteries and garrison of some 3,000 regular troops, would be suicidal. The British therefore decide to attack from the rear, despite the considerable natural obstacles. The French have left this area so lightly defended precisely because it's so difficult to attack. The target beaches are in the elbow of a huge bight, five miles deep and 15 long. Reefs and islets parallel the shore, almost as far up as the very northern tip of Mozambique. The narrow channels leading through this natural curtain wall to Courrier Bay, which forms the western coast of the narrow isthmus backing Diego Suarez, are barely a mile wide and thought to be impassable to a force of significant size, especially at night. Those channels are also very probably mined. Beyond this barrier are just a few miles of clear water between the island chain and the shore, yet it's this slit trench of an ocean approach that the British force plans to storm.

The *Franconia* has been making her usual slow time in convoy, zig-zagging every six minutes or so to avoid U-boats. It's been a trying voyage, with scurvy and skin infections breaking out among the troops. Then on 17 April the *Franconia* receives an Admiralty message that the 13th Infantry Brigade Group is to join the expedition at Durban. Convoy WS 17 arrives in Durban on 22 April, and a whirlwind of preparations for the assault begins. Cargoes are restowed, vehicles on shipboard serviced, buoys and measuring gear distributed around the ships along with charts and photos, wireless sets tuned and tested, stores reshuffled and reorganized ready for battle. Meanwhile, the grateful troops receive oranges and other fruit to clear up their scurvy. Almost immediately, though, John is called away from all this essential preparation by a summons from Captain Bertenshaw, who he finds closeted with a Rear Admiral, an Army Lieutenant-Colonel, and an Army major with no specific unit insignia on his uniform and a pronounced French accent.

"Graham, we're looking for volunteers with familiarity with these waters from peacetime, as well as excellent navigational abilities and some experience in secret operations," the Captain explains. "I understand you had considerable experience around Madagascar and cruising through the Mozambique Channel before the War, and I told the Rear-Admiral here about your exploits in the Western Desert. We need some special expertise to scout out the approaches for our attack plan. We believe you might have the right skills for the job."

The Captain coughs softly and stands back. Although he's nominally John's commander, he defers to the military officers, who step forward to complete the briefing.

"SOE has already been working on this since mid-March," the Rear-Admiral explains, bending over a chart that John instantly recognizes as the north-west coast of Madagascar. "Our plans call for our assault force to land under cover of darkness. Now, the only Admiralty charts for that stretch of coastline we have date from 1892. We have to have a fresh and accurate survey of that coast before we can risk bringing our forces inshore. That will mean approaching the shore and surveying it extensively, under false colours, at great risk of seizure and capture. For such a task, we would only ask for a volunteer, Are you ready to take this on?"

"Yes, Sir," John agrees unhesitatingly. At least this will be closer to the fighting and the killing, he thinks, even if once again it's just a reconnaissance mission, with no intentional engagement with the enemy at all. He might even get to fire a shot: at least he'll be able to do the enemy some direct damage. The presiding officer, a Rear-Admiral no less, steps forward to shake his hand, followed by the others. He's instructed to assemble his kit and be ready for departure at first light the next day. He has just time to write Farah a note:

I'm sorry, dearest, rushed once again – have only minutes to catch the post. I've been called away. You may not hear from me again for a long time, but don't despair: no matter what happens, I will be with you. I'll write again as soon as I can, I promise. Keep up your studies and don't get too bored without me. With all my love, John.

Once again, John finds himself flying at short notice, this time from Durban to Dar-es-Salaam, familiar from the old pre-war days of cruise stops at Zanzibar and Cole Porter calling on the Sultan in his palace. There he boards the vessel chosen for the task, the *Lindi*, a 60-foot schooner with an auxiliary diesel engine. After so many weeks cooped up in the iron walls of the *Franconia*, he's sailing on the open sea again. His companions on voyage are a rum lot too: a dangerous-looking South African Army captain, a gruff sergeant who admits to being a whiz at demolition, a monosyllabic wireless operator. They cross the Mozambique Channel in short order, and as they approach the western coast of Madagascar, John starts taking sightings and making notes for his survey, relaying the more important findings back to Durban over the radio. They see no Vichy vessels or aircraft during the crossing, and touch the coast at Majunga, where they pick up a couple of laconic French whites from Madagascar itself, part of the SOE team. From there, they sail up the coast to Courrier Bay, with John taking notes at every point. This stretch of the Mozambique Channel is prone to strong and unpredictable currents; John maps them at every stretch. They make landfall at Ambararata Bay, just south of Courrier Bay itself and opposite the planned line of approach for the assault force, on the night of 29 April, six days before the invasion is due to begin.

Once there, they learn that a lot of their work has been done for them. The leading SOE agent on Madagascar, Percy Mayer, a naturalized French resident, has convinced the local Vichy authorities that he can supply badly needed rice from southern Madagascar to Diego Suarez aboard lighters travelling up the coast to Courrier Bay. The Vichy naval commandant at Diego Suarez warns Mayer that Courrier Bay is heavily mined. Mayer ingratiates himself with the other local commanders, and receives guided tours of all the installations along the Bay. The original plan is for Mayer to pass this information along to the *Lindi*, lying doggo in Ambararata Bay, but the commanders of Operation Ironclad decide that enough useful information has already been gained, and that the *Lindi* itself could jeopardize surprise if discovered. After just one night, the *Lindi* is ordered to pull back and hide out in the lee of one of the offshore islets, to wait until the night of the invasion itself, when it is to show a light on Nosy Anambo, an islet 20 miles west of the main island chain with a single lighthouse, to guide the fleet to landfall. At least there John can continue his hydrographic survey and relay the information back to the fleet. His survey reveals that Nosy Anambo, the pivot for the entire operation, is one and three quarter miles to the west of its charted position, and he has just time to inform the fleet before radio silence descends.

Meanwhile, the first units of the task force set sail from Durban on 25 April, followed by the balance of the forces three days later. Operational secrecy is kept so tight that most of the assault force have no idea of their destination until a few days before the attack. Most of the convoy captains think they're heading for Mombasa. Fluctuating currents first speed up the convoy on its approach, then put the operation at risk when one force overtakes another, but finally all are assembled ready for the assault.

The main assault force of 34 ships forms up in an arrowhead formation, divided into groups, the ten Flower-class corvettes, minesweepers and destroyers of the initial mineclearing screen, Group II, comprising the barbs of the arrowhead, and the bulk of the fleet, the shaft of the arrow. Immediately behind the destroyer screen is the cruiser *Devonshire*, then the two assault transports, the *Winchester Castle* and *Royal Ulsterman*, carrying No. 5 Commando and the 2nd Battalion of the East Lancs, making up Group III, the initial landing group. Behind this first force are three more destroyers, and the main group of assault transports and Landing Ship (Tanks), Group IV; then another three destroyers, and the troopships, including the *Franconia*, and stores ships bringing up the rear in Group V. Offshore, just to the north of Courrier Bay is Group I, the covering force to defend against air, sea or submarine attack, including the World War 1 vintage super-dreadnought battleship *Ramillies,* flagship for the operation, the aircraft carriers *Indomitable* and *Illustrious,* the cruiser *Hermione,* and seven more destroyers. On its final approach, the arrow formation of 34 ships has to sail 88 miles, through unpredictable currents, between close-set reefs and islands, in complete radio silence without station-keeping signals, in the dark.

With no final countermand or contraindication, the *Lindi* casts off once more in a perfectly still evening, under a brilliant moon, to place their white light on Nosy Anambo. But placing the light on the island, with its manned lighthouse, proves impractical. Instead, they decide to drop anchor exactly in the middle of the deep channel where the oncoming ships can see them, but swirling currents in the channel make it impossible for the *Lindi* to hold steady. Worse, the only way to keep the white light shining in the right direction is for one of the crew to keep it pointed that way. John takes the tiller and fights the currents to keep the schooner on station as another crew member shins up the mast and waves a homemade torch to guide the oncoming fleet.

Alerted by the *Lindi*'s light, the three destroyers tasked with laying buoys to guide the fleet through the narrow channels, the *Anthony, Laforey* and *Lightning*, take up position and start laying their buoys around 10:00 p.m. on the night of 4 May. The bright moonlight paints the surf and outlines of the islet brilliantly, and a couple of hours later all the buoys are laid and the first minesweepers of Group II are entering the channel.

The ships of Group III make their final approach along the buoyed channel, between the little offshore islet of Nosy Hara and the even smaller islets of Nosy Belmotro and Nosy Anjombalova, with hardly a mile of sea room, and drop anchor just before 2:00 a.m. on 5 May. Due to the snarled contours of the islets and reefs, most of the minesweepers have lost their sweeps and the channels have not in fact been swept. Fortunately, the Vichy forces have not laid mines this far out. Nor do they spot any of the approaching ships, although John has a magnificent view of the flotilla from the deck of the *Lindi* as they sweep past in the moonlight. Once at anchor inside the island belt, the *Devonshire* is hidden against the backdrop of Nosy Hara, ready to give fire support to the landing. Meantime, Forces IV and V sail through the channel in their turn. The landing craft are manned and lowered as soon as their parent ships are through the channel and at anchor. The minesweepers continue to sweep ahead of Force III as the flotilla of ships and landing craft sails north up the bay, and at 03:00 a.m. a mine explodes in *Romney*'s trawl, followed a quarter of an hour later by another. Miraculously, no one in the shore garrison hears the explosion. Other landing craft from Force IV move off from their parent ships and head for the beaches further south. The *Royal Ulsterman*, following close behind, finally takes up position at the jumping-off point at 04:15 a.m. and loads its cobles with more troops. The landing craft and cobles move out, and at 04:30 a.m., No. 5 Commando and one company of the 2nd East Lancashire Regiment hit the three Red beaches and Blue beach in Courrier Bay, while the units of the 1st Royal Scots Fusiliers and 2nd Royal Welsh Fusiliers from Force IV hit White Beach and Green Beach in Ambararata Bay.

The landings come off almost without a shot being fired. Ashore, Mayer has cut the telephone wires to the battery on Courrier Bay overlooking the landing grounds, preventing it from sending a warning or receiving orders. The battery and all the Red Beach targets are taken and occupied without resistance. At Blue Beach, the landing forces encounter return fire, but the troops from White and Green beaches, advancing across the narrow point between Ambararata and Courrier Bays, are able to overrun the defenders from the rear.

To provide air support for the landings, HMS *Illustrious* launches three groups of six Swordfish biplanes to attack Vichy shipping in the bay off Diego Suarez, while HMS *Indomitable* launches Albacore bombers to bomb the airfield at Arrachart, and Martlet fighters to provide air cover for the landing parties. The first flight of Swordfish arrives over Diego Suarez and sinks the French Armed Merchant Cruiser *Bourganville*. Before this has finished foundering, the second flight sinks the submarine *Beveziers* as it tries to get under way. The planes also drop leaflets calling on the Vichy defenders to surrender. The attack on the airfield at Arrachart, meanwhile, achieves complete surprise and destroys most of the Vichy air power on the ground. The invasion force has already achieved air superiority.

At dawn, after signals that the first landings have succeeded, the rest of the assault force passes through the channel and starts disembarking the remaining troops, despite heavy seas and Force 8 winds. John takes the opportunity to rejoin his ship. Meanwhile, the landing parties from Red Beach, spurred by the relatively light resistance so far, cross the narrow isthmus and storm Diego Suarez with a couple of Bren Carriers before its dazed defenders have had time to react. At 11.38 a.m. on 5

May, the corvette *Auricula* hits a mine and breaks her back, but without casualties. At 01.54 p.m. a last holdout above the north end of Red Beach is winkled out by shellfire from the *Laforey*. After that, landing continues undisturbed until nightfall. Operation Ironclad has stormed the iron-bound coast almost without loss.

The naval base at Antsiranana and the eastern side of the island take another day of fierce fighting to subdue, culminating in a dramatic dash through the harbour defences by the destroyer HMS *Anthony* to land a party of Royal Marines on the base's jetty. By 01.45 a.m. on 7 May, Antsiranana has surrendered. Percy Mayer, betrayed by an old business associate and arrested as the first attacks begin, is liberated by the British forces, just before his scheduled execution.

Madagascar will take another seven months to conquer completely, but the rest of the campaign is a low-key, desultory affair now that the key port facilities are in Allied hands. The British sink another French submarine off Courrier Bay on 7 May, and another the next day. After the pacification of Antsiranana, the rest of the fleet sails round the tip of Madagascar and anchors in Diego Suarez bay. The *Ramillies* is torpedoed at her moorings in Diego Suarez on the night of 30 May by Japanese midget submarines, vindicating the strategic concerns that inspired the whole invasion in the first place. By this time, however, it's no longer John's affair. On 19 May the *Franconia* re-embarks its troops, and sets sail for India. The assault on northern Madagascar has finished so quickly that the 91st Field Regiment of the Royal Artillery, part of her complement, has not even had a chance to disembark its guns. It's a bad crossing for many of her cargo, and there's a long sick list on her arrival in Bombay on 29 May. By the time John sights Bombay, she's flying under a less than glamorous yellow quarantine flag, and Red Cross ambulances are waiting to cart the victims of malaria and other tropical ailments off to hospital. John's almost grateful that the censor's restrictions prevent him from writing to Farah about that. The *Franconia* returns to Britain via Durban and Cape Town, and by early

August, John is back in Liverpool.

Chapter 16

Artie initially gets a 3-A draft deferment as sole provider for his mother, and keeps playing gigs through most of December 1941, enjoying strong audience support and high poll scores in *Billboard* and *Down Beat*. Then in January 1942 his draft status is changed to 1-A, making him eligible for service. In March, he marries again, to Betty Kern, daughter of composer and lyricist Jerome Kern. This time it's a decorous affair, with the parents' approval, and by April Artie is talking to the draft board about a potential job with the USO, organizing bands in army camps. The negotiations don't work out, and at the end of the month, he enlists in the US Navy.

Artie begins his naval career close to home – as an apprentice seaman on board a minesweeper moored in Staten Island. For Artie, it's sheer drudgery of mopping decks and building shelves, although he does prove quite an apt marksman during rifle drill. After a couple of months of basic training, he's promoted to Chief Petty Officer and sent off to Newport, R.I., to form a band. The strain of trying to lick Naval material into shape induces a series of migraine attacks. Finally, Artie goes AWOL in civilian clothes and takes a trip to D.C. He manages to push his way into the office of the Undersecretary of the Navy, James Forrestal, a personal acquaintance from jazz days, and gets signed authorization to form his own band. He keeps his C.P.O. rank – because, he claims, his chief audience is not officers, but enlisted men.

Artie returns from Washington with carte blanche to pick his own musicians from the treasure chest of naval recruits. His new naval band, the U.S. Navy Rangers, includes talents like Sam Donahue on sax, Claude Thornhill on piano and Max Kaminsky on trumpet, as well as Dave Tough on drums. Many of the players have already received offers from Glenn Miller and Benny Goodman to play with their wartime bands: they turn them down for Artie. By December 1942 he has his ideal lineup assembled, and Betty Kern is pregnant with Artie's son.

In January 1943, Artie and his band ship out for Waikiki, and for five months, Navy Band 501, a.k.a. The Rangers, perform pointless military band exercises at Pearl Harbor in the morning, followed by afternoon gigs three times a week at the Breakers enlisted men's club on Waikiki Beach, then evening performances at the Pearl Harbor officers' club, interspersed with gigs at other camps around the island and on board visiting ships. The band is good enough to win the annual *Esquire* poll, but they have to endure day after day of belting out the same old favourites, with "Begin the Beguine" played time and time again, although at least by now the swaying palms and tropical splendour are real. They deliver one celebrated radio broadcast of the number, on 30 January 1943, to celebrate President Franklin D. Roosevelt's birthday. The romantic mood causes Artie some disciplinary problems, as his bandsmen get ever more involved with local girls, let alone Dave Tough's constant alcoholic binges. He's hardly ideal for the Navy command structure himself; a martinet to those below him, and resentful of those above. He has some reason: many of the Navy top brass do consider Artie's mission "silly," and he has to scrape for transportation and digs.

In early April 1943, they begin a tour of the South Pacific, first for a month aboard the battleship USS *North Carolina*, then island hopping by plane from Nouméa to Espiritu Santu, the New Hebrides and the Solomon Islands. Everywhere they play, on islands, on atolls, on shipboard, they're greeted by enthusiastic servicemen. On one memorable night, aboard the aircraft carrier USS *Saratoga* off New Caledonia, they set up their bandstand on the aircraft elevator, and kick off playing "Nightmare," as the elevator descends with them into the bowels of the ship. The crowd goes wild.

Word also gets around among the Navy brass about Artie's other unusual habits. His father-in-law later describes him as the kind of magpie intellect that gets fascinated by all kinds of nickel-and-dime knowledge, and that tendency is fully on view during his off-watches. It's not every day that you find a seaman in his bunk reading about the Riemann hypothesis. Some bright spark apparently remembers Riemann's position among the antecedents of general relativity, and somewhere Artie's records get another flag, somewhere in the vast interstices of Naval bureaucracy.

Artie and his band have plenty of unpleasant surprises awaiting them on tour. They don't get the kind of featherbedding enjoyed by Glenn Miller and his band. Ships at sea are in constant danger of attack, and more than once, Japanese bombs or torpedoes hit ships close by. The *North Carolina* herself has already fought through the Guadalcanal campaign, and in September that year is torpedoed off Guadalcanal. Onshore it's not much better. The conditions in some jungle venues are so humid that the saxophones come apart at their seams and pads rot off.

In July, Artie and his Rangers arrive on Guadalcanal. The battle for the island has in theory been over since February, but nightly Japanese bombing raids continue, and Artie and his band bunk down in tents honeycombed with bullet holes. Often they have to run straight from the bandstand to the foxholes. The Japanese are using daisy-cutter bombs, with a high enough detonation point to leave the bandsmen safe in their foxholes, but a ferociously loud bang just overhead. Artie is caught one night in a Japanese bomb run where bombs bracket his foxhole, leaving him permanently deaf in his left ear. Dave Tough and Max Kaminsky, who both came on board the band with medical waivers in the first place, both contract dengue fever. For entertainment, they have Artie's old numbers, including "Begin the Beguine," played on Radio Tokyo's *Zero Hour* programme. Artie also learns by radio of the birth of his son Steven on 30 June.

In August, Artie breaks down under the strain of the constant bombing, and wanders off into the jungle. A passing officer in a Jeep notices him and picks him up. The officer asks Artie where he's going. Artie says he doesn't know, and breaks down in tears. He's taken straight off to a base hospital and put to bed with battle fatigue.

At least, that's the official story that gets put about later. The true events are somewhat different.

Chapter 17

It's a personal war for John now, in more ways than one. There's the simmering anger and hunger for revenge still smouldering after the deaths of his parents and sister, and the devastation of his home in the Clydebank Blitz. But there's also the direct threat to the Seychelles and Farah, one of his few other remaining human ties on this whole planet that he's criss-crossed so many times. The Japanese presence in Burma and the Indian Ocean, balked for the moment after the Battle of Midway and the loss of Guandalacanal, but still a persistent menace, means that the Seychelles could be a target at any time. If Ceylon fell, the Seychelles would surely be the next domino. After his many Indian Ocean cruises, John has the strategic vision to realize that in Madagascar he was fighting to defend Farah too.

All the more frustrating, then, when his next convoy, WS 22, is another Indian Ocean passage to India, leaving Liverpool late August with over 3,500 troops aboard, and arriving in Bombay on 17 October, followed by the usual return journey via Cape Town and Freetown to moor in Liverpool mid-December. It's a relatively uneventful journey, and John has plenty of time to pine and cast his eyes east and south-east towards the Seychelles, hidden behind the curve of the ocean horizon. His stellar observations and astronomical notebooks assume the quality almost of a cycle of devotions during this period, because he's mapping the stars in her sky, chronicling the constellations that hang above her. He's careful to keep the exact details out of his letters to her, though: nothing would attract the attention of a vigilant censor quicker than navigational details. Besides, how could he explain that certain stars bring back the memory of her full breasts, her dark eyes? His parents are a fond yet bitter memory now: she is what he fights for, and the stars light his way back to her. If only he could take some leave and a passage to Port Victoria. But it's not possible. With five months in hand, however, he is at least able to work on his studies.

John spends his Christmas leave with his brother Alex and his family. His brother, one of the survivors of the Blitz, has relocated to a house in the Vale of Leven, and still travels every working day to the John Brown shipyard to work. It's not a bad place to live either: Alex has found a tolerable two-up-two-down for his wife and two bairns, and although there isn't the same sense of closeness and community as there was in Clydebank, John has to admit that it's more open, with cleaner air and a better view of the hills. It's another cold, snowy winter, with the mercury below freezing all day, and thick drifts everywhere, though the hardy Scots spare a few thoughts and prayers for the massed Russian defenders of Stalingrad. Rationing bites as hard as ever into the festive fare, but John has done his duty by the family and brought home plenty of gifts from India, including toys that enchant the children. Cloistered within the shelter of the blackout curtains, they sit by the fire on Christmas Eve and listen to the radio. For the first time, he hears Bing Crosby sing Irving Berlin's "White Christmas," and he can't stop crying, images of the dusty cotton-wool snow on his mother's Nativity scene and the drifting ashes in Clydebank flickering through his mind. It's the first time he's cried since his parents' death. All the grief, all the desolation he's carried inside since his walk through the rubble of his home, all the frustration and impotent rage, pour out for the first time. He holds on to his brother and howls uncontrollably, upsetting his little niece, who starts to cry too. Half uncomprehending, his brother hugs him and slaps him on the shoulder, thinking he's suffering from shellshock.

He also gets the Christmas present he was most hoping for, a letter from Farah:

Dear, your missing letters all came together. It is terribly difficult to write to you when I haven't had the latest reply, so I'll make up for it now. Besides, I do feel so lonely without you. I know it's strange to say it when I am with Mama and Papa and my friends here, but I feel like there is no one I can open my heart to. I so wish I could walk with you once again, even if only for an hour, and just talk. I know it may be a selfish wish in the midst of all this suffering, and your grief, you poor thing, but I can't help feeling it. I hope this letter does arrive for you in time for Christmas, my love, and I wish you all the best wishes of that season. Naturally, we don't celebrate it, but Port Victoria is full of Christmas decorations, even in wartime. I do miss those in Glasgow, though, and I look forward to one day seeing them together with you. All my love for now, darling, and Merry Christmas.

A few days later, just before New Year, all the brothers meet to lay flowers at the mass grave in Clydebank. Out of consideration for the kids, they've left the rest of the family behind, and go along by themselves. There's not much to be seen beneath the driven snow, now that many of the remaining ruins have been levelled, but they make the pilgrimage nonetheless. The flowers are the only splash of colour in a grey and white world.

January brings a sudden change to John's war, though. The strategic balance is shifting after the Second Battle of El Alamein and the arrival of US forces in the Mediterranean with the Operation Torch landings in November 1942. The Allied position in the Mediterranean and North Africa is no longer so precarious, and the spirit is far more aggressive. John's first convoy of 1943, Convoy KMF 7 out of Liverpool on 6 January, is a fast haul through the Straits of Gibraltar to Oran, now in Allied hands since the liberation of French North Africa in November. The convoy loses only one ship to a submarine en route, and by the end of the month, John is back in Liverpool via Convoy MKF 7, in time to hear the news of the German defeat at Stalingrad. Three more fast convoy runs between Liverpool and Algiers follow in quick succession, bringing stores and reinforcements for the Tunisian Campaign further west. Every stop at Algiers brings the same revelation he remembers from the *Franconia*'s cruises in peacetime: that stunning arc of white buildings around the bay, shining in the harsh sunlight, the multicoloured houses further up on the surrounding hills, and then the appalling stench as the wind from onshore brings the reek of the city on board.

John is now measuring his time at sea in weeks and days rather than months, and spending far more of it in heavily contested waters open to air and submarine attack. The fatigue begins to tell on him. The learned essays on mathematics and astronomy dry up. It's as much as he can do to try to improve his Arabic a little, even with the benefit of such frequent stops in Algiers. At least he has plenty of chances to buy oranges for his brother's family, rare treasures now back home. Then, after the fall of Tunisia in May 1943, June brings yet another change in tempo. The *Franconia* sets sail from Liverpool on 29 June as part of Convoy KMF 19, carrying troops for Operation Husky, the invasion of Sicily.

For the first time in a long time, the *Franconia* is able to dock in Malta. The Axis siege of the island has effectively ended in November 1942, after two years and over 3,000 bombing raids. The last German bombing offensive in October 1942 has met massed air defences and run up a crippling number of casualties. With the Axis unable both to keep Malta under siege and defend North Africa, the island becomes the Allies' offensive springboard for actions in the Mediterranean. Convoy protection is no longer strictly necessary for shipping headed for Malta after December 1942. Malta has in fact become quite the mecca for Allied forces.

The Allies have already captured some Italian sovereign territory, commencing with the tiny volcanic island of Pantelleria, closer to Tunisia than it is to Sicily. Subjected to intensive bombing and shelling over a month in Operation Corkscrew, the island garrison of 12,000 surrenders on 11 June as soon as the first British commandos reach shore. The nearby Italian islands of Lampedusa and Linosa surrender the next day. The Americans are convinced that invasion of the Italian mainland is irrelevant to Allied grand strategy. However, the British are eager to sustain the momentum of the Allied victories in Africa, and begin what Churchill believes will be a thrust into the soft underbelly of the Axis. General Bernard Law Montgomery moves his headquarters to Malta at the end of June 1943, followed in early July by the Supreme Commander General Dwight Eisenhower and Lord Louis Mountbatten, Chief of Combined Operations.

The Allied force for the invasion of Sicily is the largest yet assembled in the European theatre, with 2,590 American and British ships, including 237 British troopships and supply ships. As soon as the convoy is past Eire, its destination is revealed, and the troops and naval forces start to study maps and plaster models of the Sicilian coastline in preparation for the assault. John's somewhat disappointed not to be asked to join the Combined Operations Pilotage Parties scouting the landing beaches, but he has to admit that he knows Asian and African waters better than Italian ones. The convoys consolidate in Valletta harbour to prepare for the grand assault, on a larger scale than anything John has ever seen.

Spared the high seas that disrupt operations for the Canadians and Americans further west, John watches as the assembled British battleships, cruisers and other vessels open up on the Sicilian shoreline in a vast arc of flame, illuminating the smaller dark silhouettes of the landing craft heading inshore. In weather so poor as to reassure the Axis defenders that no one would attempt a landing in such conditions, the Allied forces come ashore on the early morning of 10 July, at 26 beaches along over 100 miles of coastline, meeting relatively little resistance. Airborne landings overnight by British and American paratroops and glider troops have fared poorly, with 69 British gliders ditching at sea short of their goal, and strong winds blowing the paratroops well off course. All the same, the Allies press on with a speed that fuels a false sense of superiority. A few Axis aircraft break through the supporting air cover from Malta, but not enough to inflict serious damage on the invasion force. By the evening of 10 July, the Allies have seven divisions well established ashore, air superiority over the coast, and Syracuse and several other ports captured intact.

The *Franconia* is assigned to support the landings at Augusta, further up the east coast of Sicily. The initial landing force, supported by two British and one Greek destroyer, is repelled by Italian shore batteries of the 246th Coastal Battalion, and the cruisers HMS *Uganda, Orion* and *Mauritius*, and the monitor *Erebus* move to bombard the coastal defences of Augusta the next day, driving the defenders back, while the supporting minesweepers clear the path to the port. There's a unit of Stuka dive bombers stationed just up the coast from Augusta, which makes the landing even more hazardous. The plumes of dust and smoke rising from each shellburst and the ensuing fires stand out plainly against the low coastline and the bare brown hills beyond. On 13 July the British 3rd Commando lands near Augusta to capture the bridges north of the town. The *Franconia*, carrying RAF personnel to be put ashore, is straddled by a Stuka attack, with bombs falling either side, but escapes undamaged. For the next day, the advantage swings between Allies and Italians until the invading forces finally consolidate their breakthrough, but momentum has been lost, and the Axis forces are able to re-establish a defensive line along the River Simeto. Augusta becomes a major focus for Allied resupply efforts through the stores dumps in and near the town. The aircraft carrier HMS *Indomitable*, the *Franconia*'s shield and defender during the Battle of Madagascar, is torpedoed on 16 July and forced to retire to America for repairs. The *Franconia* herself escapes unscathed once again.

For the next few days, Montgomery's forces hurl themselves against the defensive line in vain. Even the Italians, so often defeated in the Western Desert, turn out to be tenacious and effective defensive fighters. Western Sicily is cleared out by 23 July, with Palermo falling on 22 July, but the push towards northern Sicily gets bogged down along that same aggravating line north of Augusta, and the Axis forces are able to evacuate the island in relatively good order across the Straits of Messina, rescuing some 52,000 German troops and some 62,000 Italians, with much of their equipment. The Axis forces establish a further defensive perimeter around Mount Etna, which is only breached on 7 August. The first Allied units do not enter Messina until 16 August. Operation Husky, unlike the minimal losses of the Battle of Madagascar, has cost the Allies over 20,000 casualties, largely due to their failure to exploit their initial advantages, against some 28,000 German casualties and 140,000 Italians. It's a foretaste of how things will progress for the rest of the Italian campaign.

The conquest of Sicily has one unexpected consequence: on 25 July, Duce Benito Mussolini, founding father of Fascism, is dismissed from office by King Victor Emmanuel, after a vote of no confidence by the Fascist Grand Council, and carted off to imprisonment in the Podgora Barracks. Marshal Pietro Badoglio forms a non-Fascist government and secretly opens surrender negotiations with the Allies. The Maltese parade a giant effigy through the streets of Valletta on the day of his fall. Even earlier than expected, the campaign has achieved one of the brightest hopes of the British Chiefs of Staff, and knocked Italy out of the war.

John soon has other distractions to occupy him, however. He is invited by his Captain to another confidential discussion, and this time is asked if he would be ready to fly out east for a mission in Asia.

Chapter 18

John is flown back to Malta in a liaison Anson, then crammed unceremoniously into the belly of a four-engined bomber, which immediately takes off and heads east. He hasn't been told a thing about his destination, or the purpose of his mission. What is obvious is that it's very urgent. That's clear from the brisk dispatch of the air and ground crews, the bustling importunity of his handlers, all for his exclusive benefit. What has he done to deserve this?

After a brief stop at Aden, hardly long enough to run from one plane to the next, John finds himself flying over the open ocean, obviously headed south-east. Once again, there's that poignant sense that Farah is just over the horizon, a far more obviously curved horizon from this altitude. If only the mission was in that direction. When an airman comes to regale him with coffee in a thermos and sandwiches, he asks him where they are headed.

"Sorry, mate, not allowed to tell you," the airman admits as he passes him the thermos. "What I can tell you is that you can tuck in, then put your feet up, because it's going to be a long flight. Not much else to do up here anyway."

Before he falls asleep, John pens a quick note to Farah, simply telling her that he loves her and always will. He already has the presentiment that this is a far riskier, more critical mission than his previous expeditions, and this might be his last letter to her. So near to her, and yet so far, he could not let that pass without a last farewell.

The constant thrumming noise in the aircraft, hour after hour without interruption, lulls John into sleep but makes actual rest impossible. When it finally touches down, he hasn't actually slept, only dozed fitfully for hours, and both head and body ache. Once again, no one will tell him where he is, but he knows from the rough latitude and the climate that he must be somewhere in Ceylon. A jeep whisks him from the airfield to a nearby lagoon with a waiting Catalina flying boat, whose crew have broad Australian accents and whose markings he can't identify in the twilight. More hours in the air and more packaged rations follow. Finally, the Catalina touches down in clear, calm ocean between two low-lying islands, somewhere in southern latitudes, and John is led ashore along a fragile jetty to a cluster of huts on one of the islands. A few servicemen in tropical kit are lounging around, apparently quite relaxed, and one of the huts has a well-disguised radio mast protruding into the palm tree canopy overhead. John is led up the steps into the hut with the radio mast, and finds inside a room fitted out as a small headquarters office, complete with a large chart table occupying the centre. Behind the chart table are two officers, one wearing the uniform of a Lieutenant Commander in the Royal Australian Navy, the other dressed as a Captain in the US Navy. And in a chair on the other side of the chart table, looking drained and dishevelled in a US Chief Petty Officer's uniform, is...

"Good God, you're Artie Shaw," John gasps, his ingrained maritime etiquette overcome by the incongruity of the situation. The man in the C.P.O.'s uniform responds with a tired, ironic half-smile.

Artie still isn't exactly sure where he is, or why, after a sudden impromptu audience on Guadancanal with a grizzled commodore who growls at him: "Son, I understand you made plenty of complaints early on in your service that you wanted to go where the action is; well, now you're gonna get your chance," followed at once by a fast flight westward in a liaison plane. He can't figure out whether it's still the same day or the next one.

"C.P.O. Shaw is here as a representative of the US Navy, since this is a joint British-US operation," the RAN officer takes the lead, speaking the King's English without a trace of an Australian accent; John is quite sure that his uniform and his rank are a blind. "There are other good reasons for his presence as well, but we'll get to those in a moment. Before we begin, be advised that everything in this mission from this point on is top secret. You are not to divulge anything about it, under any circumstances, to anyone, including members of your families, and other officers in your branch of service, if asked, under the most extreme penalties. Is that understood?"

John and Artie both nod dumbly. Artie gets to his feet and comes to stand by John at parade rest, on the nearside of the chart table. On the table, beside a large-scale chart of the southern Indian Ocean, is a second chart of a single, roughly Y-shaped island.

"We're here: the Cocos Islands," the Lieutenant-Commander declares, disclosing their location for the first time. "Here, just over 500 nautical miles to our east, is Christmas Island. It's a British colonial territory, but it's been occupied by the Japs since March 1942. Now, Christmas Island has rich phosphate deposits, and until the occupation, it was jointly administered by the Colonial Office and the British Phosphate Mining and Shipping Company. Most of the locals ran away into the bush when the Japs started putting them to work, and the Japs haven't been able to get much phosphate out of it since, but that's not why you're here. One of the Company's former employees, still resident on the island, is this man." He slaps a yellowed photo down on the chart. "Now, I believe you're both reasonably well acquainted with spherical geometry and topology, which is one reason we brought you both here in the first place, and which means you probably know him."

Artie shrugs, indifferent. John puzzles over the image for a moment, until light dawns.

"That's Mirza Salam, the astronomer and mathematician," he realizes. "He wrote a kind letter about my paper in the *Monthly Notices of the Royal Astronomical Society*."

"Indeed." The Lieutenant-Commander responds with dry condescension. "Now, as you're no doubt aware, Dr Salam is eminent in a number of other areas of mathematics as well as astrophysics. Some of these are crucial to fundamental developments in certain areas of weapons design. Up until now, we don't believe that the Japs have put two and two together and tracked him down, but it can only be a matter of time. They've already started to share intelligence with the Germans in this field, and we know that the Germans are further ahead in developing these areas of research. Furthermore, we've received reports that the Japanese are planning to round up the population of the island *en masse*, and deport them. We can't allow him to fall into their hands."

"Your mission is to proceed to Christmas Island and extract Dr Salam, as well as any important papers he has with him, and return them to us," the American officer chimes in, without unfolding his arms.

John ponders on how much inside information the Allies must have on Japanese communications and plans to know all this, but keeps his speculations to himself.

"The rendezvous is set for 2:00 a.m. in two days' time, on West White Beach, here on the north-western coast of the island," the British officer resumes, indicating a point along the upper left fork of the Y on the detailed map. "It's a small beach, mostly surrounded by cliffs and jungle, well away from the port and the one main settlement on the island, Flying Fish Cove, here." He puts his finger on the upper right tip of the Y. "Phosphate production on the island has been at a standstill since an American sub torpedoed a Jap freighter last November, and Japanese commitment has dropped away to almost nothing. We've made contact with some of the local fugitives in the bush, and according to our best intelligence, there are only some 20 Japanese soldiers on the island. They'd take hours to get across the island to West White Beach. An incursion there has minimal risk of being discovered or resisted. Especially the way we plan to do it."

"A PBY flying boat will drop you just off the beach at 01:45 hours," the American officer takes up. "You will go ashore by small boat and rendezvous with Dr Salam and our agent. You will then return with him and any useful documents to the PBY for the homeward flight. You will avoid all contact with the enemy, and evade encounters rather than confronting enemy forces. Is that clear?"

John holds up his hand. "How are we supposed to use our mathematical knowledge, Sir?"

"He's bringing his notebooks and papers with him," responds

the phoney Australian officer. "You both know enough mathematics to identify which are the important ones, and pick those out if things go wrong. We're relying on your knowledge to leave nothing important behind."

"If you're surprised, or look to be on the point of capture, you have to kill him, and burn his books," the American adds. "His knowledge is too potentially dangerous to be allowed to fall into enemy hands. You must treat him like any agent with a poison pill in case of capture."

"Have you told him this?" John rejoins, aghast.

"No, but he knows what's at stake," the Briton continues.

"So we'll be armed?" Artie hazards.

"You'll be armed," the American confirms. "You've both been chosen because you have high marksmanship scores, as well as mathematical knowledge. And in Mr Graham's case, a strong record in inshore navigation and small boat handling. You're both qualified for the job, and we expect you to do it."

John holds up a hand. "Sir?" he asks, addressing the Lieutenant-Commander.

"Yes, Graham?"

"I remember hearing reports of mutiny or some such on Christmas Island, before it surrendered to the Japanese, involving the deaths of some British officers. Can we be sure that Dr Salam is loyal to us?"

The Lieutenant-Commander fixes him with a withering glare. "As we have already made clear, we are in contact with agents on the island. Dr Salam has assured us that he wants to help the Allied cause. We have complete confidence in him."

John subsides, seeing that it'd be useless to press the issue any further.

"If you have no further questions, you will return here at 20:00 hours for your final briefing before departure," the British officer concludes, in a tone that makes it clear that no further questions will be countenanced. "I suggest you get some sleep. Dismissed."

James and Artie turn and leave the hut, as the two senior officers turn back to their papers. Outside, it's a gem of a tropical dawn, with drifting clouds blushing pink in the first eastern rays, and golden glints off the waves. There's a clink of mess tins and a smell of cooking from another hut a little further along the beach, where the local garrison must be dishing up breakfast.

"Well, I dunno 'bout you, but rather than bunk down, I'm gonna take a swim," Artie declares, in a strong American accent that somehow John hadn't expected.

"A swim?" he echoes in amazement.

"Sure: how long you been flying?" Artie points out, with a sardonic grin. "Bet you're pretty ripe, right? And when's the last time you saw a sea without a burnt-out wreck or a warship in it? Plenty of time to sleep later."

As though to underline the point, the PBY starts its engines and drones off on its taxi run before takeoff, leaving a long white wake between the two islands.

Artie strips off his kit and runs straight down the gently sloping beach into the water, stark naked. "C'mon, what are they gonna do to us, court-martial us?" he calls back up the beach. "They're sending us to our deaths anyway." John ponders, shrugs, and follows him. Soon they're splashing and lounging in crystal clear water, surprisingly cool and refreshing in these tropical climes. John feels the ingrained filth of months wash away.

After they've bathed their fill, they lie back on the beach, drying off in the sun's early rays.

"I've been sweating in jungle heat on Guadalcanal for weeks," Artie grumbles. "When I'm not shitting my pants in foxholes, that is. I couldn't miss the chance to wash it all off."

John chuckles, looking down between their bare feet to the turquoise and amethyst sea.

"Something on your mind, sailor?" Artie raises a dark eyebrow.

"Just thinking that I've now seen what only Lana Turner has seen," John grins.

"Fuck." Artie shakes his head, appalled. "Don't tell me you're one of those."

"Good God, no."

Artie cocks his head. "A Scot, right? Well, Mr Scot, you got someone waiting for you back home?"

"I have," John nods. "You?"

Artie shrugs, with an odd, vague, faroff look in his eyes. "Yeah, I do. Or at least I suppose I do. Got a wife and a newborn son. Didn't get the news till I came out here. But you know, it seems hard to get my head around? Like I can't believe it's real, or anything to do with me. I guess that's what being under fire does to you."

"I suppose." John gazes into the waves, listening to the gentle pulse of the surf. "I lost my parents in the Blitz. Somehow I still can't believe it. My brain understands it, but my heart still refuses to accept it. It's like something undigested still sitting in my guts." He slaps his midriff, hardened by all the sparring drills.

"Hell, that must be rough." Artie sighs. "Never had that much feeling for my father. When I heard he was dead, the first thing I did? I laughed."

"That's harsh," John remarks. "I loved my father. Still love him, I suppose. He was a draughtsman. He was the one that brought me up to study, and value my numbers."

"My father always looked down on studying," Artie scowls. "It was thanks to him I started to teach myself, but only to make up all the ground I'd lost thanks to him. Been studying ever since, every spare minute. Look, I really don't know about Mirza Salam's work, but I guess you do. Is he really that good?"

James shrugs. "It's hard to say. Great mathematicians can pop up out of nowhere. Look at Srinivasa Ramanujan. I do know that he's at home across a whole range of pure and applied mathematics, not just the areas I was interested in. I guess if anyone is likely to be able to help make a big push in weapons design, he is. Wells's Carolinium, the uranium bombs in *The Man Who Rocked the Earth*, Ming the Merciless's Death Dust, someone's going to do it. Which makes me wonder, even more so with this talk of a mutiny: do you think we're here for a rescue? Or an assassination?"

Artie shrugs. "I don't see how we can know until we get there. For now, at least we're out of the front line, right? There's no sense trying to guess: you know how everything goes to shit in this war. Let's just enjoy it while we can."

The sun comes up fully over the palm trees, and the temperature starts to soar, and John and Artie put their clothes back on and retreat to the shade, to breakfast off NAAFI coffee and fresh fish caught in the lagoon. The local garrison is a platoon of the King's African Rifles, all black askaris under regular British Army officers, and their dark skins and cheerful chatter add the final touch of surreal incongruity in this charmed circle of an atoll, so peaceful and beautiful in the midst of wartime. "They're better looked after than they are in Arkansas," Artie remarks approvingly of the askaris. "And at least they ain't asking me for my autograph."

By noon, the heat and long journey have caught up with John, and he snatches a few hours of sleep on an empty bunk in one of the huts. Then he kills some time with Artie, going over some mathematical puzzles and discussing the Titius-Bode law. He's delighted to find that the New Yorker really is a gifted mathematical amateur, like him, and not some faker. The senior officers keep themselves to themselves, and John is perfectly satisfied with that arrangement. Then, around 5:00 p.m., as the sun is dipping towards the horizon, there's a noise of engines, and another Catalina, painted jet black, comes flying in from the east. "There's our ferry," Artie remarks ruefully. The senior officers come out to inspect the arrival, and John and Artie get to their feet.

The Cat touches down at the jetty and throws a mooring rope to a waiting askari. A couple of aircrew scramble ashore from the cockpit and march up the jetty. The lead airman throws an easy salute to the RAN officer and introduces himself as Pilot Officer O'Shaughnessy.

"We're a little light on aircrew today, Sir," he explains to the Lieutenant-Commander. "Left a couple of the gunners behind to make extra room for passengers. Hopefully your men know how to shoot. If we need to shoot, that is."

"They can shoot," the RAN man replies calmly, and introduces John and Artie. O'Shaughnessy barely blinks as he registers Artie's face and identity.

"Show my men your special cargo, Pilot Officer," the Lieutenant-Commander orders. O'Shaughnessy leads them under the wing.

"That there is a local boat." He points up to a dark shape slung under the wing, somewhat smaller than a 12-foot dinghy. "We've got an outboard for her on board as well. We can drop her right into the water offshore with the bomb release. Little bit trickier to resling her, but I was briefed that this is a one-night stand, right?"

"Is that thing going to throw you off balance?" the self-styled RAN man muses, looking up at the boat.

"No, Sir: got a couple of bombs the other side," the Pilot Officer grins. "Just a little extra present for the Japs."

"Very good, Pilot Officer. Get your men rested and fed, and ready for departure at 21:00 hours. We'll convene for a briefing in the command hut in 30 minutes."

Half an hour later, they sit down once again round the chart table in the main hut, this time with O'Shaughnessy and one other man who he introduces as his navigator. The Lieutenant-Commander goes over the flight plan with the airmen, then turns to the details of the beach landing.

"You'll set down about 500 yards offshore," he explains. "Our man on the beach will show a light, and that will be your signal that the boat can move in. The seaplane should remain on station offshore, to be ready for departure and to signal by flare in case of any Japanese approach from the sea. The boat will proceed to the beach, land, and collect our passenger, as well as any other documents he has with him. You are to observe strict blackout and radio silence at all times. Is that all understood?"

"We've bombed Rabaul, stalked the Jap convoys, mined their harbours, all by night," O'Shaughnessy proclaims. "This'll be a milk run by comparison."

The Lieutenant-Commander bristles at the implied

insubordination, but says nothing.

"And here's that other extra package we were asked to bring," O'Shaughnessy adds, and lays a roll of canvas down on top of the charts. He opens it to reveal a selection of weapons: a .303 Lee-Enfield rifle with telescopic sight, a silenced Sten gun with a long heavy suppressor, a Welrod silenced pistol, and other gear, including torches, fighting knives and spare magazines. "Take what you need, gents."

"I'll take the rifle," Artie declares, picking out the SMLE. John takes the Sten and a long box magazine, and slots the magazine into the feed port.

"Hold it by the canvas wrapper round the barrel when firing, and only fire short bursts," the Lieutenant-Commander counsels, almost chiding. "It heats up very fast." Strange knowledge indeed for a Navy man to have.

"If you're done, gentlemen, we're almost at zero hour," the American chips in. O'Shaughnessy rewraps the rest of the bundle and tucks it under his arm.

They troop out together to the end of the jetty. The swift, early tropical night has fallen, and the southern sky is lit by glittering, brilliant stars. No moon at least, John notes thankfully.

"Well, good luck, gentlemen, and we'll expect you back at dawn," the Lieutenant-Commander concludes, and this time he does shake hands. John and Artie get into the PBY through the big side door forward of the front wing strut. John notices a piece of nose art under the cockpit window, a girl in a black catsuit with ears and tail, "Touch Not the Cat" written in yellow below her. In the dim cabin lights, the strutted, sparred interior is a bilious green.

"We've got hot coffee the whole way," the flight sergeant put in charge of them says, pointing to the incongruous urn in the PBY's miniature galley as they make their way towards the back of the craft. "And bunks, so feel free to have a kip if you need along the way." They sit down together on the bunks, aft of the engineer's trapeze-like station in the wing root, and the flight sergeant hands them flight helmets, showing them where to plug in the intercom jacks. Once they're safely installed, he goes back forward, and after a moment, the engines overhead cough into life. John knows that the Cats are supposed to be quiet, but the racket overhead seems almost deafening, and he can't imagine how any Japs can avoid hearing them coming. There's a lurch, a feeling of motion, the whole craft sways, and then within minutes they're airborne.

Pilot Officer O'Shaughnessy may be garrulous on land, but once in the air he is all business, clipped and precise. The long hours pass. One crew member comes aft with a clipboard in his hand, and taps on Artie's flight helmet.

"Excuse me, Sir, but the crew heard who we had aboard, and wanted to ask, if you wouldn't mind, could we have your autograph?" he half yells above the engine noise. John expects Artie to object, but this time he smiles and calmly signs sheet after sheet, nine in all. The crewman nods and ducks his head almost like some hotel doorman before retreating to the forward compartments. After that, Artie lies back on his bunk and does go to sleep, rifle slung on the bulkhead in front of him.

John realizes that there's nothing to stop him slipping into the rear compartment where the waist gunners would normally be stationed, to gaze up through the gun blisters at the starscape above. He amuses himself for a while making impromptu sightings and spotting familiar constellations, closer to the southern stars than he's ever been before. If only this flight could go on forever, he muses.

But it can't. Too soon, it seems, O'Shaughnessy's voice comes crackling through the intercom. "Coming up on target, five minutes," he announces. Artie stirs, and sits up in his bunk. A minute later, the engines fall silent, and the incessant drone gives way to the rush of air against the airframe. O'Shaughnessy must have cut the engines to glide the lightly loaded plane in for the last moments before touchdown. There's a thud and a splash of water against the hull, a juddering deceleration, and within seconds the ship is down.

O'Shaughnessy turns on dim red low-visibility lamps inside the cabin. John and Artie gather up their gear as the flight sergeant comes to collect them.

"Came down right on the button," he hisses to them as he hurries them forward. "Lovely clear night outside, and no sign of any Japs."

The side door facing the beach is already open. John and Artie stick their heads out into the night air to see one crewman slide forward along the low railing round the side of the Cat to the nose, open a hatch, and lower a very maritime-looking anchor carefully into the water without making a splash. The crackling and popping of cooling metal above is the loudest sound they can hear, and further away, the hiss and wash of phosphorescent surf on the beach.

The same crewman lowers the boat from the bomb rack into the water, pulls her into the side of the hull with a boathook, then unwraps the tarp that has kept her interior dry. He lugs a small outboard motor from inside the Cat, and fixes it to her rear end. O'Shaughnessy comes down from his cockpit, holding his own small red blackout torch.

"Just ten minutes past the hour," he announces in a hoarse whisper, tapping his watch. "And look, there's the beach signal now."

Sure enough, a faint white light is flashing from the beach. O'Shaughnessy holds up his torch, blinks a reply, then turns back to John and Artie.

"We'll stay on station for the next couple of hours," he tells them. "Once you're ready, flash us twice to let us know you're coming out. Just don't be all night, okay? And try to stay quiet."

He hands them both down into the boat personally. John's nervous around the Catalina, but the floatplane seems to be no more unstable than many medium-sized watercraft. He tugs at the lanyard for the boat's outboard, and on the second try, it coughs into life. The noise can't really be loud, but it seems to echo ominously in the metal vault formed by the PBY's overhanging wing. The crewman with the boathook gives them a farewell push, and they swing out from the Catalina and head for the beach.

John watches for currents as they approach the shore, but

tonight at least, the sea seems fairly quiet. The surf up ahead is breaking smoothly and regularly on the beach in a long sparkling line that silhouettes Artie's form hunched in the bow. John glances around, fearing a Japanese patrol boat or aeroplane, but the brightest lights apart from the lamp on the beach are the stars above. In the last few seconds before they hit the beach, he cuts the engine and raises the outboard out of the water, letting the boat slide smoothly forward and crunch into the shore. They both jump out, and Artie produces the boat's own small anchor and drives it into the gravelly sand.

The dark waiting figure on the beach douses his torch and scurries up to them.

"Hello, you the Australians?" he hisses, in a strong Chinese accent. "Dr Salam up there. You follow me, we bring him down here."

That's unexpected, John scowls, not seeing fit to correct him about nationalities. He glances at Artie, and they both shrug to each other and follow the Chinaman up the beach. They reach the cliff wall and scramble up a narrow path between some razor-edged coarse undergrowth into the trees above. It's a climb of just 20 or 30 yards, and John looks back through gaps in the trees to see the shining surf beyond. He can just make out the Cat as a dark cross shape in the ocean, silhouetted against the starscape, showing no lights, and he hopes against hope that the Japanese can see no more.

At the head of the trail, at the top of the cliff, John makes out a glimmer of light between the trees. That's where the Chinaman is leading them, towards the light. As they approach, John realizes that it's the dim glow of a Tilly lamp turned down, shining through the half-shuttered unglazed window of a derelict forest hut.

"Mr Salam here," the Chinaman explains, and slips through the doorway of the hut without knocking or signalling. John and Artie follow him in, and find, in the crumbling, ruined interior, a small, spare, lean man in a suit, his white hair shining in the lamplight.

"Ah, you are my escorts?" he asks in a low voice. "Jang here has been invaluable in keeping contact with your people. Dr Mirza Salam, former engineer with the British Phosphate Mining and Shipping Company, at your service."

He steps forward and shakes hands with them both, incongruously dapper and polite in that island ruin. John notices that his suit, though bearing a few stains and tears from the walk down the forest trail, is neat and well pressed.

"Sir, we'll need to get you to the beach straight away," John responds. "Our transportation is waiting."

"Then I must ask you gentlemen to give me a hand," Dr Salam spreads his hands and indicates the floor on either side. John's heart sinks. Salam has brought down several bales of paper, each roughly the size of a suitcase, bound together with strips of blanket and hessian ropes.

"Just give me a moment, please, and we'll discuss this," he replies, and takes Artie aside to confer just outside the door to the hut.

"Look at that; do you think we can make it now?" he asks.

Artie purses his lips and looks at the bundles. "If you say we can put them in the boat, we can. I'd reckon two trips down to the beach tops to carry that lot. And if things get rough, we can fire them up on the beach as well as we can here."

"That's what I thought. I'll stay here with the man; you and the Chinese take the first load down. We can't leave him alone here: who knows if he might change his mind and try to run?"

Artie looks ready to argue the toss, but finally nods and turns to Jang. Together, they each heft a bundle under each arm and head back toward the beach.

"My name is Graham, Sir," John begins hesitantly. "You wrote some very kind words about my paper, 'Al-Khwarizmi's Revision of Ptolemy's Geography and the Determination of Indian Ocean Coordinates'."

Oh yes, I remember: fine piece of work," Dr Salam smiles. "You have my compliments, young man. You made excellent use of your findings at sea. My own point of observation is far more static, I'm afraid."

"I hope things haven't been too rough for you."

Dr Salam sighs and shakes his head. "Not too pleasant for a man of my years, but tolerable. The Japanese have bothered us little so far. As for the silliness of the mutiny, God is no friend to murder. I am frankly rather glad to be away from all of that, even if it means hiding in the forest."

"You never thought of getting away earlier?" John asks. "Off the island, I mean?"

"Oh, not at all, not at," the older man chuckles spryly. "It was the attempt by scientists here in 1922 to test Einstein's Theory of Relativity by viewing a solar eclipse from the island that spurred me to take my mathematical studies more seriously. It would seem pure ingratitude to leave after that. I even built a little observatory up there on the hillside. It was such a good place to study the beauty of the works of God."

Dr Salam's eyes are so round and innocent, his demeanour so confiding, that John feels any mistrust would be an impertinence. There's a bustling noise outside that makes him turn and unsling his Sten, but it's just the Chinaman pushing back in, wiping his face. There's only two more bundles left now to go down to the beach, and a small suitcase that John presumes must contain Dr Salam's personal effects. Pushing his head through the doorway in the dim light, Artie grins at John, then his grin fades, and he freezes.

From somewhere along the trail leading off east along the cliff top comes a voice, and a flashing light. Jang springs at the Tilley lamp and snuffs it. Immediately, everybody crouches down below the level of the window sills. John cocks his weapon, pulse beating in his ears louder than the surf below. The voice cries out again, in Japanese, and a torch beam splashes against the wall of the hut. By its light, John glances round the room. Dr Salam is squatting on his haunches with his hands over his ears, eyes wide and fearful. Jang has drawn a long blade, probably a machete, and is crouched ready to spring at the doorway. Artie is half through the doorway, his rifle up, and John watches him swing the barrel back and forth, between the open window facing onto the trail and Dr Salam.

Now the noise of footsteps and muffled conversation is plain outside. Thank God, there don't sound to be too many men. John can make out the flashing torch beam and moving shadows through the half-shuttered window and the broken slats of the shutter. The beam plays along the side of the hut. Then he sees a shadow fall across the shutter and a dark shape obscure the holes in the slats. He half rises to his feet, holding the Sten by the canvas barrel wrapper as instructed, aims through the shutter, and fires.

The muffled burst tears through the wooden slats, clattering loudly enough inside the hut despite the silencer. John stands up and steps to the window, and sees just outside, eye to eye, a glistening oriental face, eyes round and shining in the torchlight, caught in a moment of absolute terror. Then the Japanese topples over on his back, still holding the torch in his hand, showing the three dark holes in his belly.

Artie darts round the side of the hut. The torch in the dead man's hand is shining its beam up vertically into the forest canopy, and by its light, John can make out another Japanese fleeing down the trail, trying to unsling his rifle as he goes. Artie puts his own rifle to his shoulder, squints through the sight, takes aim, and snaps off a shot that catches the soldier right between the shoulder blades, knocking him down. That one rifle shot seems to echo off the hillside and fill the night, rolling away across the miles of forest.

"That's torn it," John gasps, and pulls Dr Salam to his feet. Jang slips out of the hut and follows Artie to the dead Japanese, making sure. John hefts a bundle of papers and puts his Sten back on his back, focused on the documents again now that the immediate danger is out the way.

"Sir, we have to get down to the beach, now," he urges Dr Salam. The doctor needs no encouragement. He grasps his suitcase and follows John out the door, with one fearful gaze down the trail at the two dead Japanese.

"No more," hisses Jang, extinguishing the torch. "Hurry now, not much time."

John almost reads satisfaction in the set of Artie's jaw as he slings his rifle and picks up the other bundle of papers.

Together they head back down the cliff trail to the beach, with John supporting the aged doctor when he stumbles on the steep path. On the beach, they crunch across the shingle, then sling the remaining bundles into the boat. The beach is still deserted, and now that the echo of the rifle shot has faded, the loudest sound is once more the breaking of the surf.

John flashes his torch out towards the waiting plane, hands Dr Salam into the boat in the manner he learned from so many beach excursions with Cunard's guests, then turns to help Jang in.

"I get away now," Jang says, shaking his head. "Go hide in jungle with others. You no worry. Just get away now."

Together they recover the boat's anchor and push her down the beach until she floats free. Once John and Artie are aboard, Jang gives her a final push, then turns to hurry up the beach. John watches him go until his dark form is indistinguishable against the treeline, then lowers the outboard into the water and starts the engine.

The dash out to the waiting Cat takes almost no time, but every moment John feels the prickling sensation between his shoulders like a target painted on his back for a rifle bullet. Artie keeps shaking his head. "I think that shot did something to my ear," he mumbles, cupping his hand against his ear and tapping it. Dr Salam's form is rigid, hands crossed across his body, clearly petrified. Although he can't be sure, John thinks he sees one light glimmer far down the coast to starboard, then another.

"Shit, we thought you were goners when we heard the rifle shot," gasps the flight sergeant when they reach the shelter of the Cat's wing. "Captain was just about to start the engines and get us out when we saw your light. Are you all okay?"

"Yes, but get us airborne now," John snaps. "Only, make sure to get those papers out of the boat."

The bemused airman helps John and Artie toss the bundles aboard the Cat. Then they help Dr Salam to step gingerly aboard. As they do, the twin engines overhead cough, and the props start to rotate. The crewman lets out the seacocks in the now-empty boat, weighs anchor, and the Cat starts moving before the outer door is closed.

O'Shaughnessy swings her round in a wide arc before beginning his takeoff run. John can't help but think at every moment of the phosphorescent wake on the water, pointing out their course like an illuminated arrow for whoever wants to look. The Cat gets airborne without any disturbance or gunfire, though, and within moments they're back on the same blind, droning flight through the darkness, sneaking westward in the night towards safety. The flight sergeant helps Dr Salam into a bunk, and Archie flops into the opposite one. John crumples on the hull beside the door, buries his head in his hands, and starts to sob uncontrollably, just as he did in his brother's house.

The flight back passes without incident, and the Cat arrives just after dawn, as expected. A party of askaris is waiting at the jetty with jerry cans of fuel, and the Cat resumes its flight with Dr Salam and his papers aboard almost as soon as they are refuelled. Artie goes with them, accompanied by the mysterious US Captain, and the last that John sees of him is a quick salute before the Cat starts its engines and pulls out of the lagoon. The Lieutenant-Commander is busy patting him on the back and congratulating him, but he can never remember afterwards what the senior officer said. Within a couple of hours, another Catalina, this time in brighter RAAF livery, is there to pick him up and whisk him off north. As they leave, he contemplates diving off the jetty into the inviting sapphire waves, and swimming all the way across the Indian Ocean to the Seychelles and Farah.

Chapter 19

The Cat whisks Artie and the other passengers to an air base on the north coast of Australia. Dr Salam spends most of the journey closeted with the US Navy Captain in the navigator's cabin, engaged in hushed, urgent conversations over papers on the chart table. Once they touch down on the Australian shore, he has time for a farewell handshake and a thank-you before the captain rushes him off to a waiting destroyer on the quayside. Seems that the US was very eager to get him on American sovereign territory, even if it's a warship.

   A PBN Mariner is waiting for Artie, to fly him back east to the Solomons, straight back to Guadalcanal. He knows it's useless to protest, but clings to his rifle with both hands, all the way home, and refuses to let go. Once he's back on the island, he's taken to the hospital and put to bed, and warned under the threat of direst consequences not to tell anyone what really happened during his absence. Dr Salam's knowledge, whatever it is, is so critical and so sensitive that everyone is supposed to stick to the cover story of hospitalization. The whole operation was so evanescent, so surreal that Artie can't think what to say about it anyway. In retrospect, it seems easier to dismiss it as a secret private performance or overnight engagement, just another gig.

   In any case, he doesn't have to fake battle fatigue. His state of nerves is obvious. Artie and his band are pulled out of the firing line and sent off on a tour of Australia and New Zealand to support the US troops serving or on R&R there, as well as the locals. In New Zealand, it's already winter, and quite a different experience to performing in the tropical hell of Guadalcanal, with better food and far better girls. The band arrives in Auckland at the end of July, and tours military and civic venues for the next couple of months, concluding with an American Red Cross dance in Auckland Town Hall on 1 September organized in honour of Eleanor Roosevelt, the First Lady, on her own morale-building tour round the South Pacific theatre. Artie is mainly impressed by the sobriety of the local listeners, who often greet the end of a set with reverential silence, instead of the wild applause from American audiences. It's the same in Australia, where the band goes next. "Australian audiences are appreciative, but not as demonstrative as the Americans," he tells the local press. Even so, at Rockhampton the audience is jitterbugging in the streets, and one venue is a stadium seating 50,000. It's a major moment for Antipodean jazz, especially in New Zealand. It's also, Artie claims later, the only time he cheated on any of his wives. There's one other macabre incident. On a DC 3 flight around northern Australia, Artie hears a Japanese-accented voice come over the intercom: "I see you, DC; but I haven't got time for you now. I'll catch you on the way back." Artie looks out the window to see the Japanese fighter before it flies away.

The exhaustion of touring and the months in combat conditions have taken their toll. The whole band is declared unfit and put on board a single Liberty Ship to return to the US. Despite the dangers of an unescorted voyage in wartime, the ship makes its journey home without interference. Artie arrives back in San Francisco on 11 November, and kisses the dock as soon as he gets onshore.

Home shores and safety do not bring a recovery, though – at least, not immediately. In November 1943 Artie is hospitalized in the Oak Knoll Navy Hospital outside Oakland, underweight, depressed and with recurring migraine headaches. He's allowed a brief Christmas furlough with his family, but almost immediately returns to the hospital. For some of the time he's kept under psychiatric observation.

Artie is granted his medical discharge from the Navy in February 1944. His band plays on as the US Navy Liberation Forces Band, touring Europe and other venues, with his books but without him. Artie settles with his wife and new child in a house in Beverly Hills, close to his parents-in-law, but it's not easy for him to adjust to civilian life, where people complain about rations in queues, after his experience of the privations and suffering in the Pacific, while his father-in-law is industriously filling their new Tudor-style family home with

Chippendale and Sheraton.

Artie's readjustment isn't helped by his continuing royalties and earnings, which mean that he doesn't have to go out to work for a living and reintegrate himself into society. Most days he lies around the house, or drives aimlessly round California. He starts a course of psychoanalysis, five mornings a week. He makes his first recording since his discharge in June, for the Armed Forces Radio Service, but it's hard for him to put a new band together. With a war still on, most of the available talent tends to be junkies or people otherwise disbarred from serving. His family life also isn't going well. Artie walks out on his son's first birthday party at the end of June 1944, and separates from Betty a few weeks later; within a couple of months they are divorced. His wife is awarded sole custody of their son until he reaches age six. Artie keeps the mock-Tudor mansion at 906 North Bedford Drive, complete with tennis court and swimming pool.

By October, Artie has pulled together enough motivation and focus to assemble a band. He credits his intensive sessions of psychoanalysis for this. The new ensemble has talents like trumpeter Roy Eldridge, pianist Dodo Marmarosa, guitarist Barney Kessel, tenor saxes Herbie Steward and Jon Walton, trombonist Ray Conniff, and junkie drummer Lou Fromm. This time it's to be a band without strings, with a new book of arrangements or rearrangements of his old standards, rewritten without the string parts by trombonist/arranger Harry Rodgers. Artie and Conniff start working together on new arrangements and mutes for the four-man trumpet section to take advantage of the leaps in trumpet technique during the 1940s – backed by a lush and mellow trombone quartet. In the fall of 1944 he also resumes recording for RCA.

Artie also starts dating Ava Gardner, although for the first eight months, the dates are purely platonic. She is still a bit-part actress at this point, waiting for her big break, but has gained some vicarious prominence through her brief marriage to Mickey Rooney, dissolved in 1943. Whether or not she helps Artie pull himself together, or whether he is able to date her because he's already done it, many credit her with his recovery. He also starts to entertain a roster of literary guests: his old sparring partner Robert Benchley, as well as S.J. Perlman, William Saroyan, Gene Fowler and Dorothy Parker. Sometimes this leads to a weird disjuncture between Artie's intellectual interests and his Hollywood glamour lifestyle, when at one instant he's engaged in intense discussions with one or other highbrow buddy, and the next moment swapping kisses with some glamorous starlet.

Musically, Artie repeats the same approach he tried earlier, and creates a new Gramercy Five with Roy Eldridge, Dodo Marmarosa, Barney Kessel, Lou Fromm and Morey Raymond, to play alongside his big ensemble, and to give him room for the more spontaneous, freeform playing he can't do with the bigger outfit. Eldridge's presence causes trouble more than once, however, as racial prejudice resurfaces back in the States. On one occasion, he's not allowed into a venue in San Diego where the band is due to play, and told to "get out of here, n-----, if you know what's good for you." Artie explodes at the culprits and gets Eldridge in to play a storming set. Later, though, when the pressure of prejudice starts to affect Eldridge's playing, Artie docks his pay. Eldridge protests and pulls a knife on Artie, who tells him "if I'm not your friend, who is?" and advises him to leave America, for a less prejudiced venue like France.

Artie tours with his band through the end of 1944 until March 1945. Despite their popularity and musical success, the band starts to lose bookings, owing to a falloff in enthusiasm for big band music. In June-July 1945 he and the band record 17 times in the Hollywood RCA studios, yet conflict between Artie and Eli Oberstein at RCA, his nemesis from previous lawsuits, winds up the relationship soon after. The end of the war in August 1945 doesn't affect Artie's life particularly, except for the continuing falloff in audiences. The returning generation of servicemen, having lost their youth in the war, are apparently more interested in starting families than hanging around in dance halls. All the dynamics that supported the swing era, including the war itself, are falling apart, and solo singers like Frank Sinatra rather than bandleaders are the wave of the future.

Still, other areas of Artie's life are going better. Artie and Ava Gardner marry on 17 October 1945. Thanks to him, she begins to take correspondence courses to improve her mind and enrols in the University of California. However, she also starts to drink. Artie can't control his intellectual aggression, his propensity for put-downs of his less gifted partners. He doesn't show much respect for movie stars, despite his propensity for them. He tells Ava that movie acting has nothing at all to do with talent, but is all about key lights and cheekbones. His inheritance from his father apparently runs deep. Artie dumps her one year and one week after the marriage. Soon after the divorce, Ava gets the first big screen break that takes her to stardom, with *The Killers*.

In 18 November 1945, with gigs drying up and only a few radio and recording engagements on hand, Artie dissolves the band. His later verdict on his 1944-45 band is unsparing. He describes the postwar band as essentially a pickup group formed to make money: fine, forward-looking musicians in themselves, but not enough to keep him on track with them. He grows bored quickly, and walks aways from the ensemble, as he did in 1939.

Other audiences find much more lasting value in the recordings that survive from that period. Roy Eldridge's incandescent talent is forgivingly disciplined and sympathetically edited in Artie's arrangements. Their sound is perfectly captured in their June 1945 RCA recording of "These Foolish Things." But Ray Conniff is called up for service in early 1945, and he and Artie never work together again. "I worked very hard and earnestly with this band, with all my musical skills," says Artie later, "but by this time the joy and fun of it had gone."

Chapter 20

John follows the same route back to the Middle East by Catalina and bomber, and is slipped back aboard the *Franconia* almost without anyone noticing. The Captain has apparently been briefed on the secrecy of his mission, and has made up appropriate explanations for the rest of the crew. No one else seems particularly curious: It's wartime, people come and go all the time, for all kinds of reasons. Furthermore, the *Franconia* is on shorter routes now, with more frequent ports of call, making intermittent absences easier to explain away.

John is keen to put the experience behind him as well, for more personal reasons. He can't get the frozen, petrified face of the Japanese out of his head. His anger and his lust for revenge has blown out like a light. Now he's simply horrified at himself. He ended a life with one casual, unthinking twitch of his finger, without even seeing the face of his victim until the deed was already done. He's no better than the German aircrew who dropped the bombs on his parents. All life, any life, Farah's, his, can be cut short bloodily, brutally, so easily, so arbitrarily, unthinkingly, unseeingly, in the blink of an eye, with the twitch of a finger. And he can't tell anyone. He can't share the experience with his crewmates because of the cloak of secrecy. He has no bonds or unit to support him, no reassuring senior officer to tell him that it's all just the cost of war and that he did the right thing standing by his comrades. He's lost any appetite for secret missions, for sneak attacks, for getting closer to the enemy and drawing blood with his own hands. He no longer wants to leave his ship and seek out more excitement. All he wants to do is get his job done and serve out his time.

Luckily for him, the *Franconia*'s next series of voyages is correspondingly pacific. Early in October, the *Franconia* sets sail from Liverpool in great secrecy, escorted by three destroyers and three corvettes, and accompanied by the escort carrier HMS *Fencer* and a screening force of five more destroyers as part of Operation Alacrity, the Allied occupation of the Azores. The *Franconia* carries Air Vice-Marshal Sir

Geoffrey Bromet, commander of the mission, and supporting RAF personnel. Portugal has been determinedly neutral throughout the War, but has maintained military cooperation with Britain, bolstered by the 600-year-old Anglo-Portuguese Alliance. In 1943, with a more successful and ambitious Anglo-American alliance making forceful overtures, António Salazar, the Portuguese dictator, accedes to an Allied request for air bases to close the Azores Gap, the open Atlantic waters between Bermuda and Gibraltar, beyond the range of Allied air cover and a favourite killing ground for the Axis U-boat offensive. The Allies may be gradually winning the Battle of the Atlantic, but March 1943 alone sees 120 merchant ships worldwide sunk by U-boats, and Churchill in particular is in no mood to risk losing the "tonnage war." In the aftermath of the Battle of Kursk and the fall of Mussolini, the Nazis are too preoccupied to launch their own deterrent invasion plan against Portugal.

The *Fencer* carries a formidable anti-submarine force of six Walrus floatplanes and four Swordfish torpedo bombers, but the convoy encounters no difficulties, perhaps because it's sailing at the nominal invitation of the neutral Portuguese government. It arrives on 8 October after a week's untroubled sailing, at Angra do Heroísmo, to offload the contingent of RAF personnel comprising the new 247th Air Group, part of some 3,000 personnel from all three services who arrive to build the airfield on Terceira Island that becomes known as RAF Lagens. Only four days later does Winston Churchill announce to a surprised House of Commons that he has invoked the Windsor Treaty of Eternal Alliance with Portugal to launch Operation Alacrity. Salazar does not actually sign the final accord giving his formal consent to the arrangement until 17 October, but by then the facts on the ground are already well in place. The whole affair is redolent of the pacific, but hardly welcome, occupation of Iceland.

John is quietly pleased that he's helped in an operation to safeguard merchant shipping, after so many merchant sailors have already lost their lives. He's also glad that it's bloodless –

not a consideration that would have occurred to him a few months ago.

Construction continues over the next few months, as Lancasters, Yorks, Wellingtons, Hudsons and Flying Fortresses fly in and start their 500-mile sweeps from the island airfield. The first U-boat kill out of the Azores follows on 9 November, but by that time, the *Franconia* is already back in Liverpool, after a side trip to Alexandria and Algiers to pick up over 3,600 troops for the journey home.

The *Franconia*'s next trip to Algiers, departing Liverpool on 13 November to rotate troops in and out of the Italian campaign, brings over 4,100 troops home for Christmas by early December in Convoy MKF 26. John isn't to join them, alas. The developing plans for Operation Overlord require a massive draft of American troops to be shipped over the Atlantic, and the *Franconia* sets sail after just a week's rest on 16 December, bound this time for New York.

For John, it's a double retrospective, of the *Franconia*'s departures from Manhattan in the halcyon days of cruising, and of his own earliest apprenticeship aboard the *Alaunia*, plying the North Atlantic passage. The Atlantic crossings in those days weren't in convoy with escorts under the constant threat of torpedoes, but the smell of the sea, the cold spray, are the same. Even with such a short passage, it inspires reflection, especially with Christmas to spend alone in New York in the wartime winter of 1943. John doesn't brood: he enjoys the cafes and bars, so much less constrained by rationing than London, he takes in Cole Porter's latest film musical (*Something to Shout About*), he celebrates Christmas in Times Square. But he thinks, a lot.

The return journey from New York in Convoy UT 7, carrying over 4,500 troops of the US 4th Division as part of an overall shipment of 50,000 GIs for the war in Europe, takes just over a week, from 18 to 29 January, despite the rough weather that leaves many of the soldiers seasick. John takes a late Christmas leave as before, with his brother and his family in the Vale of Leven. This time, he does manage to enjoy himself, and to lay a wreath for his parents on the Clydebank mass grave, with more sincere grief and spontaneous, healing tears. The hills around the Vale of Leven and the Coats Observatory also allow him to further his studies, especially while the blackouts are diminishing the urban skyglow. Although the war is far from over, there are enough indications that the end is in sight for John to seriously start considering his plans for peacetime – if he survives. He decides that he wants to resume his plans to take up academic study of astronomy and its history, if that opportunity is available for him after the last all-clear. He shares the plan with Farah by post, and she writes back enthusiastically. She has had none of the excitement and terror of war to divert her from the drudgery of administrative work at Port Victoria, and is eager to grab at any prospect of post-war advancement and adventure. The idea that they would do it separately just doesn't even occur.

In February 1944, John is back to the Mediterranean for a trip to Taranto in Puglia, site of the first British landings on the Italian mainland in September 1943. The Allied advance up the boot of Italy towards Rome has proven slow and costly, rapidly turned into the campaign of missed opportunities, and troops are being fed piecemeal into the meat grinders of Anzio and Monte Cassino, but forces still need to be reshuffled for Overlord and the push into France. The *Franconia* arrives back in Liverpool on 22 April as part of Convoy MKF 30, carrying over 4,000 troops and 4,000 items of mail, including John's own latest letter to Farah. The next Mediterranean run, to Oran, takes just three weeks in May. With the Mediterranean practically an Allied lake by now, it should be a milk run. But the *Franconia* develops engine trouble in her port engines. Limping home on only one engine, she manages only 10-11 knots, which is still adequate for the convoy's average speed of 8 knots. All the same, she badly needs repairs, and on her arrival in the Clyde on 29 May, is laid up for over four months for repairs off Garelochhead, the port facility at the north end of Gare Loch.

Victory depends so often upon seizing the moment, exploiting the opportunity, stepping into the breach. It privileges the instinct for absolute contingency possessed by the great commanders, among them John's namesake, James Graham, the Great Montrose. It also means, though, that a lost opportunity makes all the difference. John has missed the boat for D-Day. It's been obvious for months that landings in France are not far off, and the long-awaited Second Front in Europe is about to open. The landing craft flotillas and Landing Ship, Infantry crews have been training day and night, in all weathers, under live fire, for months. John could not be shoehorned into the plans at this late hour. Other Royal Navy and Merchant Navy volunteers are fighting and dying on Juno, Sword, Gold, Omaha, before his application for transfer of duty has cleared the sorting office.

   Rather than waste his time while the *Franconia* is laid up, John furthers his studies. His paper has opened doors in academic circles, and he exchanges letters, and later, personal meetings, with William Smart, Regius Professor of Astronomy at the University of Glasgow. Professor Smart's own background as a former naval officer, and author of the *Admiralty Manual of Navigation* and other standard volumes on navigation for the Armed Forces, helps cement the bond, and the two spend long afternoons together in the draughty, half-empty halls of the University, discussing problems of spherical astronomy and celestial dynamics, while the radio crackles with reports of further advances in Normandy. When he can, John takes the train the short distance to Edinburgh, reproved all the way by posters asking "Is Your Journey Really Necessary?", to further his Arabic.

   News of the invasion of southern France in August in Operation Dragoon disappoints him, for he realizes he's been passed over for service in that campaign as well, but the fact is that the war has become professionalized and institutionalized now, no longer a place for amateur heroics. John reflects that he's an idle cog in the machine that is at least free to spin by itself for a while longer. He delves deeper into the history of the House of Wisdom and Baghdad's lost golden age, the crucible of learning fuelled by the new medium of paper imported from China, the repository of classical culture and the sciences while Europe slumbered through its Dark Ages, the earliest formulations of the true scientific method in the hands of Ibn al-Haytham and his peers. He watches Alexander Korda and Michael Powell's *The Thief of Bagdad*. He sees how pasteboard and garish the cinematic pyrotechnics are, how superficial and cliched the oriental trappings, but he can't help but revel in it and see himself in that setting.

Repaired and back in service, the *Franconia* sets sail for New York in early October as part of Convoy UC.40A. Once again, the entire passage there and back takes just under a month. On 12 November, she departs on another voyage to Taranto, one that deprives John of his festive season, the "Merry Little Christmas" of winter 1944-45. Throughout that critical period, as the Allies fight the Battle of the Bulge and fend off the last abortive German attempt at a counter-attack against the impending conquest on two fronts, she shuttles between Taranto and Port Said. After their return to Liverpool on 6 January 1945, though, the routine changes. Many of the *Franconia*'s old luxury trappings are taken out of storage for refitting. Rumours start to circulate that she is being spruced up for an important passenger, a very important passenger indeed.

Chapter 21

By 1944 Cole Porter has followed *Panama Hattie* with three more popular yet uninspired shows: *Let's Face It!* (1941) with 547 performances, *Something for the Boys* (1943), with 422 performances, and *Mexican Hayride* (1944), with 481 performances. Wartime guarantees the audiences, but Cole's muse is not so dependable. The latest developments in music theatre have rather left him behind. Ever since the triumphant success of *Show Boat* in 1927, with music by Jerome Kern and lyrics by Oscar Hammerstein II, appetite has been building for the so-called "book musical," where the individual songs and production numbers are subordinated to the overall unity of an often serious drama. *Oklahoma!*, from Rodgers and Hammerstein, has massively reinforced the trend, running for a total of 2,212 performances from its Broadway debut in March 1943. It's a smash hit far beyond even Cole's successful wartime productions, and representative of the new taste. It also takes a very different approach to the one that formed Cole's style, the old Broadway tradition of revues and frivolous musical comedies. The *New York Daily News* states that: "*Oklahoma!* really is different – beautifully different. With the songs that Richard Rodgers has fitted to a collection of unusually atmospheric and intelligible lyrics by Oscar Hammerstein 2nd, *Oklahoma!* seems to me to be the most thoroughly and attractively American musical comedy since Edna Ferber's *Show Boat*." Always both his own composer and lyricist, Cole has a new standard to work to, and he finds it hard to compete.

   Cole is already feeling dispirited when Billy Rose, fresh from his success in producing the smash hit *Carmen Jones*, invites him to contribute the music and lyrics for a revue, *Seven Lively Arts* in 1944. The plan is to celebrate the seven "lively arts" of music, theatre, opera, ballet, radio, painting and concerts, in a gently satirical spoof of show business. Moss Hart, returning to work with Cole, writes the book, Salvador Dali contributes set designs, and some of the ballet music is provided by Igor

Stravinsky. Rose decides to create an extravaganza in the manner of the old Ziegfeld follies. Bert Lahr and Benny Goodman are among the stars lined up for the cast, while other jazz stars Teddy Wilson and Red Norvo are playing in the orchestra.

Tryouts begin on 24 November 1944 at the Forrest Theatre in Philadelphia, with performances sold out. Advance ticket sales for New York soar to $500,000. However, squabbles between the cast, and the generally unfinished nature of the whole production, doom the show before the Broadway opening on 7 December 1944 at the Ziegfeld Theatre. "'Seven Lively Arts' no longer is what it started out to be, a gentle satire on show business and the allied trades, but it has become a gigantic, sprawling spectacle," declares the *New York Times* review, which also remarks "Cole Porter has written the music for the show, and the tunes definitely are not his best." One of the numbers, significantly, is titled "Dancin' To A Jungle Drum (Let's End The Beguine)." Even drawings by Dali in the theatre lobby and free champagne aren't enough to save the show. *Seven Lively Arts* runs for 183 performances, a reasonable run at this point in Cole's career, and loses $150,000.

Significantly, the review adds: "Probably the nearest approach to the old Porter style – he will regret having written all those good ones in former years – is 'Ev'ry Time We Say Goodbye'." On the day of the show's Broadway opening, Cole gets a note from Dr Albert Sirmay, his music editor at Chappell, which reads: "I myself have a personal affair with your song 'Ev'ry Time We Say Goodbye.' It chokes me whenever I hear it . . . It is a dithyramb to love, a hymn to youth . . . It is not less a gem than any immortal song of a Schubert or Schumann . . . This song is a classic and will live forever."

First sung in the show by Nan Wynn, "Ev'ry Time We Say Goodbye" is an instant classic. Called a jazz standard, it seems to have very little in common compositionally with jazz, but is closer to Cole's finest balladeering of the past couple of decades. The composition is almost monotonous in its simplicity, in the manner identified with Cole's work ever since

"Night and Day." But it's also a mark of his ability that he manages to hold the monotony for just long enough without sapping the audience's patience. He also manages to keep lyrics that occasionally flirt with pretentiousness just close enough to simple and natural everyday speech, in the best manner of enduring popular songs. He pinpoints "the change/from major to minor" in exactly the same place in both the music and the lyrics, with the chord change from Ab to Abm. Some critics call the song untypical of his output, but if it is, it's hard to imagine a single greater expression of his genius. The endless internal rhymes, the toying with monotony, the fusion of simplicity with sophistication, let alone the major/minor interplay, they're all there.

The Benny Goodman Quintet makes the first recording of the song on 16 November 1944, for release in January 1945, after which it rises to No. 12 in the charts.

There's no love song finer
But how strange the change
From major to minor
Ev'ry time we say goodbye

could stand as much of the secret of Cole's musical career, as well as one of his last outstanding hits, the touch of orientalism infused into his music. It's not quite his own farewell to composition or even to success, with shows like *Kiss Me Kate* still yet to come, but it does come close to a swan-song. Even with the war so near its close, it also serves as the memorial for many wartime romances and bereavements, for those busy dying the whole way.

A photo from 1945 shows Cole smiling and indomitable as ever, seated at his piano in double-breasted suit and bow tie, with a carnation buttonhole. You may dismiss his work as the tinsel confections of a spoiled mommy's boy whose wealth and prestige shielded him from anything like the real danger and tragedy faced by his audience, but you can't deny that, unlike Cole himself, his songs have legs.

Chapter 22

On 11 January, the *Franconia*'s new master, Harry Grattidge, one of the few survivors of the disastrous sinking of the *Lancastria*, is summoned to the Admiralty Building at Whitehall and informed by the First Sea Lord, Sir Andrew Cunningham, that she is to be made ready to leave for Sevastopol in six days' time, carrying Prime Minister Winston Churchill and his entourage to a meeting with his Russian and American counterparts at Yalta, on the south-eastern end of the Crimean Peninsula. Sevastopol, on the opposite side of the Peninsula from Yalta, has been chosen as the anchorage for the British mission because Yalta itself is heavily mined, and the Russians have unreliable charts of the minefields. Turkey has allowed no British ship through the Dardanelles into the Black Sea since 1939, but the *Franconia* is nominally a civilian ship, granted passage by treaty, and the Turks will hopefully turn a blind eye to her.

Yalta, annexed from the Ottomans by the Russian Empire in 1783, originally rose to prominence as a fashionable 19th-century retreat for the Russian gentry, including Leo Tolstoy and Anton Chekhov, whose White Dacha still stands. After the Russian Revolution, the Communists turned it into a health resort for the working classes, and Stalin used it as his summer residence until its occupation by the Germans in November 1941. By the spring of 1944, the Germans have been driven out of the region.

Meanwhile, Franklin D. Roosevelt has been pressing for another grand summit of the Allied leaders since the November 1943 Tehran Conference, hoping to secure one before the November 1944 presidential elections. In the event, he wins re-election for an unprecedented fourth term, his declining health concealed from the electorate, and shifts his focus to a meeting in a neutral Mediterranean location. Churchill seconds him, seeing the whole shape and structure of post-war Europe clamouring for review. His informal "percentages agreement" with Stalin in Moscow in October the previous year for spheres of influence has no official standing, and something formal and public has to be decided between the three powers. The Soviet Union is rolling up swathes of Eastern European territory: Bulgaria, Romania, Poland, Hungary. In Greece, British forces have joined right-wing government units in open battle against Communist groups, with Roosevelt's endorsement. Stalin agrees to Roosevelt's proposal, but insists that he has been advised by his doctors not to travel, and in late December proposes Yalta as an alternative venue. His fear of flying undoubtedly plays a part. Roosevelt is therefore treated as the nominal host for the conference. He accepts Stalin's proposal of Yalta, but is concerned at the prospect of a flight over Italy and the Balkans: Churchill proposes Malta as a staging post. "No more let us falter! From Malta to Yalta! Let nobody alter!" he telegraphs Roosevelt on New Year's Day. In the event, Roosevelt voyages by sea from the US to Malta.

Winston Churchill already has an established routine for wartime travel on Cunard liners, laid down during his transatlantic trips on the *Queen Mary*. He and key members of his entourage occupy First Class suites, restored as far as possible to pre-war standards, with service to match, including fresh flowers daily. His suite has to be sealed off from the rest of the ship, and conference and map rooms provided, as well as separate dining quarters and staff facilities. Marines guard his quarters, and he is provided with all the alcohol he desires, whatever the arrangements for the rest of the ship. The *Queen Mary*'s chef has become a personal favourite, and Churchill insists on his transfer to the *Franconia* as soon as the plan for Yalta is formulated.

Five days of frantic refitting restore the *Franconia* to something of her former glory. The PM's suite is installed forward on A deck, with dark green upholstered armchairs and a green bedstead. As well as her new luxury conference facilities, the *Franconia* has also been equipped with a powerful wireless station to support the delegation's communications needs. Cranes are fitted to support the contingent of 46 vehicles needed to supplement Soviet deficiencies in land transport, as well as six boats and two amphibious DUKWs. As a cover in case of some last-gasp sabotage or air attack by the Third Reich, heaters are installed and anti-freeze oil ordered, to give the impression of a planned voyage north into the Arctic.

The *Franconia* has been given the code name "Disraeli" for the duration of the whole mission; the code name for Sebastopol is "Buchan." For the Operations Section of MI5, entrusted with the security of British VIPs travelling abroad, this is Operation Argonaut, and Major H.F. Boddington is assigned to accompany the PM's party to oversee security arrangements. A Russian proposal that the *Franconia* should also bring back 2,000 Soviet prisoners captured by the Allies while fighting for the Axis has been turned down.

Boddington interviews John briefly before the *Franconia* sets sail.

"I understand that you participated in missions with the Long Range Desert Group during the North African campaign, and undertook clandestine reconnaissance work for the landings at Madagascar," the Major begins, sifting through a slim manila file on his desk. "Served with Force 136 in South-East Asia as well, and killed a man."

"I'm not at liberty to discuss such operations, Sir," John responds, remembering the strictures placed on him after the Christmas Island mission, and suspecting that this impromptu interview is some kind of test.

"Very good." The major sucks his lip. "Experienced in small craft handling, clandestine landings and inshore navigation. A good shot too. Well, we may have need of your talents, Graham. Should the occasion arise, we'll let you know."

He closes the file, dismissing John wordlessly. Cognisant of the great responsibility that might be placed on him, John still doesn't feel it in his heart. All he feels is fatigue.

A 13-coach overnight train arrives at Liverpool docks from London on the morning of 17 January 1945, carrying some 120 senior officers, diplomats, clerical and subordinate staff, and Royal Marines guards for the *Franconia*. That afternoon, she sets sail from Liverpool bound for Malta and the rendezvous with Churchill himself, taking the long way round Northern Ireland to steer clear of submarines. The ship makes slow passage at first, thanks to heavy winter weather which forces the Captain to slow her to avoid damage to the vehicles on deck. At Malta, they find that plans have changed. The Russian hosts have now prepared accommodation at Yalta for Churchill and his immediate entourage, who will fly in to Saki in the Crimea for the onward road journey to Yalta. The *Franconia* will only accommodate the Prime Minister towards the end of his stay. However, her freight of supporting officials and her radio station will still be essential to the success of the British mission, as, in the words of the official Cunard description, "a veritable floating annex of Whitehall."

The airstrip at Saki is readied, and around a hundred RAF personnel fly in to set up facilities for the British and American arrivals. The *Franconia*, meanwhile, passes through the Dardanelles, carefully made up to disguise anything military and official. Her munitions and vehicles on deck have been tarped over, her military passengers are dressed uniformly in chalk-striped suits, bought wholesale at the Captain's initiative from a Liverpool tailor. The Turkish authorities raise no objection to her passage. Afterwards, she navigates through a blizzard off Balaclava, and threads between unrecorded minefields and uncharted wrecks, to moor on 30 January at the devastated city of Sevastopol, only liberated in May the previous year and still in ruins. The city also has practically no facilities, not even derricks for unloading the cars vital for Churchill's planned drive from Saki to Yalta. After intense negotiations and some hard bluffing, the Captain finally secures a fleet of barges from the Russian Admiral of the Port to offload the vehicles, just in time to meet Churchill's flight. That's John's responsibility, managing the crush of lighters round the *Franconia*'s hull, jostling between the ice sheets in the freezing water.

Churchill and Roosevelt arrive on 3 February by plane from Malta, and drive for five hours over mountainous territory to

Yalta. The town has the ghostly atmosphere of any seaside resort in winter, exacerbated by wartime damage. Much of Yalta outside the areas cleared for the conference is still mined. Churchill describes it as "the Riviera of Hades."

The US delegation is installed in the Livadia Palace, a summer resort for the last tsar, Nicholas II, which becomes the plenary venue for the entire conference, given Roosevelt's nominal role as host. Churchill and the British delegation are assigned the Vorontsov Palace, five miles away, originally designed in an odd fusion of mock-Tudor and Moorish style by Edward Blore, the architect of Buckingham Palace, and the former residence of Field Marshal von Manstein during the German occupation. Both palaces are filled with "furniture carried with extraordinary effort from Moscow," as Churchill says, with 1,500 railway coaches journeying four days to bring the bedding, furniture and carpets. They are also infested with bugs, of the technological and the entomological kind. The PM's entourage taps *Franconia*'s surgeon for DDT to eradicate the lice, but he's unable to provide this. Stalin arrives at Yalta one day later by armoured train. The famous photo session at the opening of the conference captures the three most powerful men in the world, *pace* the disintegrating amphetamine addict in the Führerbunker, seated together in one place for the last time to preside over the division of the spoils. Three leaders, temporary allies in the same war, sharing more power over more of the population of the planet than any white men from the same Christian tradition have ever had in history – or ever will again. And two out of the Big Three are bitten all over by bedbugs.

Roosevelt's overriding priority for the conference is to secure Russian participation in the war against Japan, which is still expected to cost millions of lives before victory. His resolve and command of detail, however, are challenged by his deteriorating health. Churchill and the other participants in the conference are shocked by how feeble he has become, in body and mind. By January 1945 he is hardly able to sign his name, and sleeps on average 12-14 hours per day, often dozing off in the middle of crucial discussions. He is hardly in a good state to play a weak hand against Stalin, no matter how strong the forces at his back.

Churchill is immediately focused on Poland, and the challenge of trying to secure some kind of guarantee of free and fair elections to support the non-Communist Polish groups against Stalin's Lublin Committee. Stalin is equally focused on Poland, to achieve the opposite. He claims that the Soviet Union wants to see "a mighty, free and independent Poland," not least because "the Russians had greatly sinned against Poland." It is partly thanks to that statement that Churchill believes, or at least accepts, his promises that the Soviets will allow free and fair elections in Poland, and the 150,000 or so Polish troops fighting for the Allies across Europe will be able to return in safety to a free country. Roosevelt is anxious to leave with "some kind of assurance to give to the world." Stalin's verdict to Soviet Foreign Minister Vyacheslav Molotov is: "Never mind. We'll do it our own way later."

Roosevelt negotiates with Stalin separately on the issue of Soviet involvement in the Far East. Churchill is shown the resulting agreement afterwards, for his signature. Germany is divided into its post-war control zones. Poland is repartitioned, losing its territory east of the Curzon Line, and receiving territory taken from eastern Germany in compensation. Stalin observes "that there were no Germans in these areas, as they had all run away." There is little in practice that the Western Allies can do to alter Soviet actions in the areas already under their control. As US attendee and presidential aide James F. Byrnes said after: "it was not a question of what we would let the Russians do, but what we could get the Russians to do." Stalin, meanwhile, makes no effort to support the Communist insurgents in Greece.

Yalta does at least confirm Soviet participation in the proposed United Nations formulated at the Dumbarton Oaks Conference, with a secret agreement on the principle of veto voting on the Security Council, and Soviet acceptance that not all of its Soviet Socialist Republics can become UN members.

Churchill's discussion of the proposed United Nations includes the caveat that he cannot agree "to any British territory being made the subject of a system under which it would be open to other Powers to make criticisms of the work which we had done in our Colonies, and which called upon us to justify our standard of administration." The veto principle, as Stalin argued the previous October, also gives Britain the chance to resist American efforts to revitalize China by returning Hong Kong, and other decolonization initiatives. The Big Three have at least confirmed the principle and structure of an international, multinational order.

John gets his chance to join the motorcades from Sevastopol to Yalta, to marvel at the splendour of the Vorontsov Palace, and to join in the convivial lunches at the British mess. There, he catches sight of Stalin, small, dainty, even hesitant, perfect confirmation of the dictum that the world's worst tyrants are overcompensating little men. He sees Roosevelt, bent over, sunken-cheeked, clearly gravely ill. And he visits the Map Room, where the whole panorama of the war is spread out across every square inch of wall space, in brilliant relief.

All three leaders leave Yalta promptly after the close of business on 11 February. Churchill insists on packing up and leaving the Vorontsov Palace the same evening. His motorcade arrives at the *Franconia* around midnight, to be greeted by Captain Grattidge alone; John and the rest of the crew have been ordered to stay out of the way. All the same, a cheer goes up as the PM comes on board, and he responds with his V for victory salute to the crew craning to catch a glimpse of him through the portholes. Almost the first thing he asks for on his arrival is a fumigating machine.

Once the PM is on board, the atmosphere of the *Franconia* is transformed. The aides, officers, diplomats and secretaries run to and fro to keep up with the flow of business, "like abstracted White Rabbits whose timepieces had betrayed them," as the Captain recalls later. The aides tend to be young, because few older men can keep up with Churchill's extraordinary energy. The radio station is kept busy by a constant flow of dispatches.

Unlike King George VI, Churchill has never been one to apply wartime rationing restrictions to himself and his family, and the catering on the *Franconia* reflects this. The larder has been fully stocked for his arrival, with fresh game and plentiful hock. The first lunch on board, with Anthony Eden and Vyacheslav Molotov, includes dressed crab, roast beef, apple pie, Liebfraumilch, gorgonzola and port. Churchill's late-night fare includes partridge cocotte and a bottle of Liebfraumilch, and the chef and stewards furnish him before bedtime with a tureen of chicken broth, kept warm overnight in his stateroom pantry.

While in Sevastopol, Churchill visits the tomb of Lord Raglan, the battlefield of Balaclava and the memorial to the British dead of the Crimean War, noting the devastation of the modern city. For John, it's like the pre-war sightseeing cruises of the *Franconia*, only with a vastly different class of passenger. A very fussy one too: Churchill complains of any noise on the ship, and the Captain closes down the Card Room to accommodate him. All the same, Churchill telegraphs his wife to compliment the ship – and carelessly deprecate its original crew: "We are taking another day of rest here on this most comfortable ship, with its *Queen Mary* staff." Others in his entourage find it "comfortable to the point of luxury." Onshore in Sevastopol, droves of grey, hollow-eyed slave labourers, all German and Romanian POWs, are toiling ceaselessly in the rubble to repair the shattered city.

On his last night aboard, Churchill addresses the crew. Mispronouncing the Captain's name, he then says: "You have made a vital contribution to the historic conference just ended . . . you have carried here and accommodated signal personnel and communications which have made it possible for me to keep in constant touch with the progress of the war ... the rapid unloading of this vast number of vehicles and equipment under the most difficult conditions reflects credit on all concerned. Thank you all. I have asked the Captain to enable those of you who may be so disposed to splice the mainbrace tonight. Now I wish you all the best of luck; when you get home, you may really feel that you have played a part in what may prove to be one of the milestones in the German war." At half past nine on the morning of 14 February, he is cheered off the ship on his way to the airfield, Greece, Egypt and home. All John feels is the sense of anticlimax.

The RAF contingent at Saki, Staging Post 150, sails home on the *Franconia* with the remainder of the diplomatic party. By 5 March she is back in Liverpool, bearing the gifts that the Russians sent for Churchill: seven kilos of caviar, 72 bottles of Russian champagne together with 18 of vodka and nine of liqueur, four cases of oranges and a case of lemons.

Chapter 23

John has one more voyage to make on the *Franconia* before peace breaks out. On 31 March 1945 she leaves from Liverpool for Halifax, harking back once again to the very start of his career at sea. Just a few days after her return to Liverpool on 28 April, Germany surrenders unconditionally.

Already back with his brother's family in the Vale of Leven, John celebrates VE Day in Dumbarton, watching the pipe bands march down streets hung with bunting and Union Jacks, saltires and Lions Rampant of Scotland. They talk of returning to Clydebank, but there's no urgency, no reality to that discussion: their lives have moved on now and their priorities are elsewhere, and that former home is a burned-out shell of what it once was. John has laid his plans already, during the hiatus in his service last year, and is ready to act on them as soon as he can. The war meant the death of his parents, and he wants no more part of it. Before the *Franconia* can be reassigned to the Far East to support the tail end of the war against Japan, the news of the dropping of the A-bombs on Hiroshima and Nagasaki, followed by Japan's surrender, raises his hopes even higher – and awakens some disquieting reflections. Was that what Dr Salam had been studying? Did his own brief excursion to Christmas Island help to bring that about? Who can ever know?

The end of the war doesn't mean the end of service, but John is ready to use every lever he has to bring his own career at sea to a close. Thanks to the wartime Minister of Labour and National Service, Ernest Bevin, British servicemen have been fairly well acquainted with the outlines of the national demobilization plan since September 1944. University students and academics are both among the favoured categories for demobilization. Government pressure on universities to expand the number of places available for students has been a constant ever since post-war policy became a real goal. John has a powerful advocate on his side in the person of Professor Smart, with his deep Admiralty connections. He unashamedly uses the

Professor's influence to secure early demobilization, prior to joining the University as an actual student. After all, the Admiralty and the country will continue to need astronavigators and astrophysicists in the dawning age of atomic science and atomic warfare. It's a powerful argument that John's ostensible superiors find impossible to resist. After decades of service, Cunard is sorry to let him go, but service bureaucracy still overrules company considerations, with the *Franconia* still under government control. Before the autumn is out, he's demobilized, with his Certificate of Discharge from Merchant Navy Service, his light blue discharge book, and his demob jacket with government issue flannel trousers. He keeps his service uniform as a memento, packed neatly away in a suitcase.

John's pay as a merchant seaman is only half the equivalent in the US services, but he has still built up a fair reserve during wartime. That's enough to buy him passage on one of the first Indian Ocean voyages that becomes available. Cunard is considerate of its former personnel, and grants him cheap passage as far as Mombasa. Surrounded by relocating refugees and former service personnel making their way home, John is once again back in his first days at sea, in cramped basic accommodation, but he would rather be nowhere else. He's no longer the one responsible for guiding the ship: he's just a passenger now. He no longer wants that responsibility, or that life, not now his eyes have been lifted to the heavens.

At Mombasa, he changes ships to an even smaller, dirtier little steamer, the best available for crossing to the Seychelles in the immediate post-war Indian Ocean. She offloads gleeful RAF servicemen from the seaplane depot at St Anne, on their own way home after serving, before taking John on board. He's only brought a couple of cases with him: after the strictures of wartime voyages, he's grown used to travelling light, and he's there with a single fixed purpose.

The slow steamer takes a couple of days to cross from the African mainland to Port Victoria. That gives John time to freshen up a little and look at himself in the mirror, his heart in his mouth. No longer the dapper young officer in uniform: just a bookish-looking civilian in a plain jacket. Then he goes up on deck to watch the piers of Port Victoria come into view, backdropped by the familiar green hills. There's no more grey naval vessels in the harbour: already the docks are returning to the colours and rhythms of peace. Just dun buildings, blue water, black and brown faces, green palms. And, standing on the end of the quay, a small figure in white.

Chapter 24

Cole Porter enjoys a few final successes post-war. His excruciating 1946 biopic, *Night and Day*, with Cary Grant starring as possibly the most incongruous Cole Porter imaginable, at least confirms him as an American cultural icon, and the score wins an Academy Award nomination, mostly on the strength of all its old Cole Porter numbers. Collaboration with Orson Welles on *Around the World* in 1946 brings no more success than did the salad of big names in *Seven Lively Arts*. But *Kiss Me Kate* in 1948 turns out to be his late masterpiece, and a demonstration that Cole can match and best the format of the new book musical. *Kiss Me Kate* goes on to be Cole's only musical ever to run for more than 1,000 performances on Broadway, and wins the first Tony Award for Best Musical.

Afterwards, Cole's career resumes its uneven downward course. *Can-Can*, opening on Broadway in May 1953, is a moderate artistic and commercial success, running for 892 performances. His stage and film work produces some more isolated hit songs in tepid settings. But in 1952 his mother dies, followed two years later by his wife. In 1958 he loses his long rearguard battle against the damage to his legs, and has his right leg amputated and replaced with an artificial limb. It's as though his creative gift has been amputated as well. He never writes another song, and spends much of his time closeted in his Waldorf Towers apartment, summering in California. He dies in California of kidney failure on 15 October 1964.

Chapter 25

Artie Shaw has a long and full life after the war's end, but produces comparatively little music. He continues to record with session musicians through the late 1940s, usually opting for a larger ensemble with strings. In 1953 he's forced to testify before the House Un-American Activities Committee over his former Communist sympathies. In July 1954, he tours Australia again, this time with Ella Fitzgerald. At the conclusion of the tour, he gives up playing the clarinet, saying: "I have taken the clarinet as far as anyone can possibly go." He later says that his compulsive perfectionism would have killed him if he had continued. In 1983 he briefly comes out of musical retirement, performing and recording many previously unperformed arrangements, but by 1987 he has ceased performing and conducting again.

Rather than continue with music, Artie returns to his earlier love of writing. He publishes an autobiography, *The Trouble With Cinderella: An Outline of Identity*, in 1952, followed by a trio of short semi-autobiographical novels, *I Love You, I Hate You, Drop Dead!*, in 1965. He continues to write short stories for the next couple of decades. Up until his death, he works on another voluminous autobiographical novel, *The Education of Albie Snow*, a 1,900-page manuscript which he describes "a sort of *Siddhartha*, a musical *Siddhartha*," that remains unpublished to this day.

Artie also continues his habit of serial monogamy, marrying *Forever Amber* author Kathleen Winsor (1946-48), actress Doris Dowling (1952-56) and actress Evelyn Keyes (1957-85). With Doris Dowling, he begets Jonathan Shaw. Ironically, both of his sons achieve some renown in their own right: Jonathan as celebrity tattooist; Steven as a collector of fine quality guitars, amassing a superlative collection which is later donated to form the Gallery of Iconic Guitars at Belmont University in Nashville.

Artie's favourite twilight occupations include target shooting and fly fishing. He dies of diabetes on 30 December 2004 in

California. Until his dying day, he never speaks of the incident on Christmas Island.

Chapter 26

Epilogue

The *Franconia* is released from government service in 1948. Restored to something of her former glory, she resumes passenger service in June 1949, carrying many post-war refugees and immigrants to Canada. She is finally retired in 1956, sold to the British Steel & Iron Corporation and broken up in 1957 in Inverkeithing, close to her birthplace on the Clyde. Her successor on the Canada route, RMS *Ivernia*, is renamed *Franconia* in her honour in 1963.

In 1946, German emigre artist Max Beckmann paints his pictorial interpretation of "Begin the Beguine." Centre stage is a pair of dancers, the man in evening dress, the woman in an elegant shoulderless version of a siren suit, but the male dancer and the two supporting figures, a clarinetist and a cigarette girl, are crippled and mutilated. Sinister birdlike figures perch behind the dancing couple, and a headless fish carcass rots between their feet. The song's title is on a board at bottom right. "The great orchestra of mankind lies in the city," Beckmann writes at one point, and: "From the starting point of the present I look for the bridge that leads from the visible to the invisible." "Begin the Beguine" stands as his reflection on America, the post-war world and its mass society, as well as the confinement of the human spirit on the material plane.

Cole Porter is buried near his birthplace, in Mount Hope Cemetery, Peru, Indiana. The large ovoid memorial stone bears simply the word "Cole."

Artie Shaw is buried in the Pierce Brothers Valley Oaks Memorial Park in Westlake Village, Los Angeles County, California. The memorial tablet bears a poem by A.C. Greene, "The Soul of the Song":

> He taught the clarinet to think
> Not just to sing.
> To explore the music it was making,
> To let the fingers probe and find

The hidden places,
The crevices of meaning and emotion
A good song has -
But must be found and captured
By some divinity or other,
A melody that cannot just be played,
For nuances and grace notes
can't be chartered,
The secret tempos and their keys
Can only be discovered
By a mind that is listening for the soul
The manuscript does not display.

In Sydney, in the Rookwood Muslim Cemetery, stands a double memorial plaque over two graves laid side by side, bearing the following inscription:

John Kenneth Graham	Farah Ayad Graham
Scholar of Islam and	
the history of science	Economist and diplomat
March 1910 – May 1995	April 1918 – May 1995

For those who do good there is good reward and more besides, neither gloom nor humiliation shall cover their faces. They are the people of the Garden and in it they shall abide.

Also Available from Roswell Publishing

Non-Fiction

An Introduction to Magick – Mozinah the Seer
Paranormal Forensic Archeology: Crime Scene Residuals and Ghostly Witnesses – Jonathan Williams, MA
Phantom Vibrations: A History of Ghost Hunting – BR Williams
Send in the Congregation – Rachael Gilliver
Skin O' Our Teeth – Rachael Gilliver
The Mysterious Wold Newton Triangle – Charles Christian
The Human Element – Rachael Gilliver
You Are Not Broken – Rachael Gilliver

Fiction

Death of a Doppelganger – Paul Mackintosh
Letters From Montauk – Rachael Gilliver
The High Price of Fame – Rachael Gilliver

Poetry

A Box at the Back of the Junk Shop – Kate Garrett
Black Ballads – Paul Mackintosh
Mozinah's Book of Fairy Tales – Mozinah the Seer

Printed in Great Britain
by Amazon